RANEY

**Center Point
Large Print**

Also by Clyde Edgerton and available from
Center Point Large Print:

The Night Train

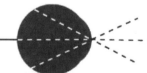

**This Large Print Book carries the
Seal of Approval of N.A.V.H.**

RANEY

CLYDE EDGERTON

CENTER POINT LARGE PRINT
THORNDIKE, MAINE

This Center Point Large Print edition
is published in the year 2012 by arrangement with
Algonquin Books of Chapel Hill,
a division of Workman Publishing.

The text of this Large Print edition is unabridged.
In other aspects, this book may vary
from the original edition.
Printed in the United States of America
on permanent paper.
Set in 16-point Times New Roman type.

ISBN: 978-1-61173-419-5

Library of Congress Cataloging-in-Publication Data

Edgerton, Clyde, 1944–
Raney / Clyde Edgerton.
pages ; cm
ISBN 978-1-61173-419-5 (library binding : alk. paper)
1. Married people—Fiction. 2. Southern States—Fiction.
  3. Domestic fiction. 4. Large type books. I. Title.
PS3555.D47R3 2012
813′.54—dc23

2012001367

I am grateful to my mother and father, Truma and Ernest Edgerton, and to others in my family, especially Oma Crutchfield, Lila Spain, and W. C. Martin, for giving me those wonderful gifts, family stories, over and over for as long as I can remember.

To Susan

PART ONE
Blood Kin

LISTRE, NORTH CAROLINA
APRIL 18, 1975

FROM THE *Hansen County Pilot*:

BETHEL—Mr. and Mrs. Thurman A. Bell announce the engagement of their daughter, Raney, to Charles C. Shepherd of Atlanta, Georgia. Mr. Bell owns the Hope Road General Store and the family attends Bethel Free Will Baptist Church. Raney graduated from Chester F. Knowles High School where she was in the school band and various other activities. She attended Listre Community College.

Charles Shepherd, the son of Dr. and Mrs. William Shepherd of Atlanta, is the assistant librarian at Listre Community College. Dr. Shepherd is a college professor, while Mrs. Shepherd is a public school teacher.

A June 7th wedding is planned at Bethel Free Will Baptist Church. A reception will follow in the education building.

The couple plans to honeymoon at Myrtle Beach and live in Listre at 209 Catawba Drive.

1

WE GET MARRIED IN TWO DAYS: CHARLES and me.

Charles's parents are staying at the Ramada— wouldn't stay with any of us—and today me, Mama, Aunt Naomi, and Aunt Flossie ate lunch with Charles's mother, Mrs. Shepherd. And found out that she's, of all things, a vegetarian.

We ate at the K and W. Mrs. Shepherd wanted to eat at some place we could sit down and order—like a restaurant—but Aunt Naomi strongly suggested the K and W. She said the K and W would be more reasonable and the line wouldn't be long on a Thursday. So we ate at the K and W.

I got meatloaf, Mama got meatloaf (they have unusually good meatloaf—not bready at all), Aunt Naomi got turkey, Aunt Flossie got roast beef, and Mrs. Shepherd, Mrs. Shepherd didn't get any meat at all. She got the vegetable plate.

When we got seated Mama says, "I order the vegetable plate every once in a while myself."

"Oh, did you get the vegetable plate?" says Aunt Naomi to Mrs. Shepherd.

"Sure did," says Mrs. Shepherd. "I've stopped eating meat."

We all looked at her.

"I got involved in a group in Atlanta which was

putting together programs on simple living and after a few programs I became convinced that being a vegetarian—me, that is—made sense."

Somehow I thought people were *born* as vegetarians. I never thought about somebody just *changing over.*

"What kind of group was that?" asks Mama.

"Several Episcopal women. I'm originally Methodist, but—"

"Naomi!" says this woman walking by holding her tray. "Good gracious, is this all your family?" Her husband went ahead and sat down about three tables over—picked a chair with arms.

"It sure is," says Aunt Naomi. "Let me introduce you. Opal Register, this is my sister-in-law, Doris Bell." (That's Mama.) "You know Doris, don't you?"

"Oh, yes. I think we met in here one time. Right over there."

"And this is her daughter, Raney, who's getting married Saturday."

"Mercy me," says Mrs. Register. She had on big glasses with a chain, little brown curls on the top of her head, and too much lipstick. "You're at the start of a wonderful journey, honey," she says. "It was thirty-seven years for me and Carl the twenty-first of last month. I hope your journey is as happy and fulfilling as ours."

"And this is Mrs. Millie Shepherd, the

groom's—groom-to-be's—mother. She's up from Atlanta, Georgia."

"Atlanta!" says Mrs. Register.

"And this is Flossie Purvis, Doris's sister. And ya'll, this is Opal and Carl Register," said Aunt Naomi, pointing toward Mr. Register who had started eating over at his table. He smiled, with food in his mouth. You couldn't see any though.

"Atlanta!" said Mrs. Register again. "You don't know C.C. Lawrence, do you?"

"No, I don't think I do," said Mrs. Shepherd.

"C.C. works at one of the big banks in Atlanta. He got a law degree and a business degree—one right after the other. His mama and daddy didn't think he'd ever finish—and them working at Liggett and Myers. He went—"

"Opal," Mr. Register calls out. "Sit down and eat."

"Well, nice to have met you," said Mrs. Register. "Good luck on that wonderful journey, honey," she says to me.

When Mrs. Register was out of hearing distance, Mama says, "Mr. Register just had a prostrate operation and I don't think he's recovered."

"Prostate," says Aunt Flossie.

"Is it?" says Mama. "Prostate? Oh. You know, I've always liked him better than her. She always makes so much out of every little thing."

The conversation went from the Registers to

15

prostrate operations back around to eating meat.

"You know," says Aunt Naomi, "once in a while I've gone without meat, but I got so weak I thought I'd pass out."

"Well, that happens a bit at first," Mrs. Shepherd says. "But after a few days that usually goes away. It's a matter of what you get used to, I think. The body adjusts."

"I'd be afraid I couldn't get enough proteins," says Mama.

"Oh, no," says Mrs. Shepherd. "There are many protein substitutes for meat. Beans— soybeans, for example—are excellent."

"My next door neighbor, Lillie Cox, brought me some hamburger with soybean in it," said Aunt Naomi, "when I had the flu last winter, and it tasted like cardboard. She's always trying out the latest thing."

"I couldn't do without my meat," says Mama. She was fishing through her tossed salad for cucumber—and putting it on her plate. "I'd be absolutely lost without sausage for breakfast. Cole's sausage. The mild, not the hot. Do they have Cole's in Atlanta?"

"I don't think so. I really don't know."

"Do you get the patties or the links?" Aunt Naomi asks Mama.

"The patties—Thurman don't like the links; they roll off his plate."

We all laughed. Even Mrs. Shepherd, so Mama

stretched it out. "Every time we go to Kiwanis for the pancake supper he'll lose one or two links. Because of the way he eats his pancakes—pushes them all around in the syrup. Last time one rolled up under the edge of Sam Lockamy's plate, and for a minute there we couldn't find it. Then Sam swore it was his."

"I guess you have less cholesterol if you don't eat meat," says Aunt Naomi.

"There are health advantages," said Mrs. Shepherd. "And also our women's group has been concentrating on how eating less meat can help curtail hunger in the third world."

"On another *planet?*" says Aunt Naomi.

"Oh, no. Developing nations," says Mrs. Shepherd. She finished chewing and swallowed. "Developing nations."

"What I don't understand," says Aunt Naomi, "is that if they don't eat their own cows, like in India, then why should we send them ours? They wouldn't eat ours, would they? Or maybe they *would* eat American meat."

"We wouldn't send meat to India, of course; we'd send grain and other staple goods. The fewer cows we eat the less grain we'll need to feed cows, so there will be a greater grain surplus."

Aunt Naomi blew her nose on this Kleenex she had been fumbling with. She had a cold. She can get more nose blows on one Kleenex than anybody I ever saw. She always ends up with this tiny corner which she slowly spreads out, then blows her nose into.

We'd finished eating so I said, "Aunt Naomi, you get more nose blows out of one Kleenex than anybody I've ever seen in my life."

"I probably won't be able to sing Sunday," she said. She sings in the church choir. "This cold just drags on and on and on."

"Ain't it nice the way Raney and Charles play music together," says Mama to Mrs. Shepherd. I was relieved to get off the meat subject.

"Yes, it is," says Mrs. Shepherd.

"I think it's wonderful," says Aunt Naomi.

"They sound real good together," says Aunt Flossie.

Music is what brought me and Charles together. He plays banjo and collects old songs from the mountains. When I sang for the faculty at the college Christmas dinner he was there— he's the assistant librarian—and he came up afterward and complimented my singing. He was real nice about it. And has been ever since. Charles is the kind of person who is real natural around people—and is smart as he can be.

Then I met him again when I went to the library to check out a record. They have a good collection, thanks to Charles. One thing led to another and the first thing you know we're playing music together. We've had three or four performances. Kiwanis and such. Charles calls them gigs.

"Charles sent me a tape," says Mrs. Shepherd. "You two sound really good together. You have a beautiful voice, Raney."

I thanked her.

Charles is learning to sing too. We harmonize on two or three songs. He's improving gradually. He plays good banjo. He don't *look* like a banjo picker, but he sounds good.

"I don't know what I'm going to do without Raney singing around the house, and helping out with Norris and Mary Faye," says Mama, looking at me.

"Mama, I'm twenty-four years old," I said.

There's a big gap between me and my little brother, Norris, and sister, Mary Faye. Norris is eight and Mary Faye is eleven. Mary Faye picks on Norris all the time, but sometimes he deserves it.

"How many children do you have, Mrs. Shepherd?" says Aunt Flossie.

"One," says Aunt Naomi.

"Please call me Millie," says Mrs. Shepherd. "All of you," she says, and smiles. "You too, Raney, if you're comfortable with that. I have only one," she says. "Charles is the only one."

2

Y<small>OU WOULD THINK A MAN COULD GET</small> married without getting drunk, especially after I explained that nobody in my family drunk alcohol except Uncle Nate, who was in the Navy in World War II, but got burned in combat on over fifty percent of his body, and caught pneumonia and had to be discharged from the Pacific. He had to stay in the hospital for three and a half months. Now he has asthma spells.

Uncle Nate comes to our house in a taxi at any hour of the day or night, drunk, cussing his former wife, who's dead—Joanne. And when I say drunk, I mean so drunk he can't get up the front steps without me and Mama and sometimes the taxi driver helping him. And smell?—Uncle Nate I'm talking about—whew. A sweat-whisky smell that lingers in the house as solid as flower smells at a funeral—lingers long after Mama's undressed him, got him in the tub, and piled his clothes on the back porch. And the thing is, he don't ever get asthma when he's drunk.

Mary Faye and Norris have to stand there in the middle of all that, being influenced in no telling what ways.

When Uncle Nate's sober he's my favorite uncle. I love his stories about when he was growing up with Mama and Aunt Flossie and

Uncle Norris (who lives in Charlotte) and their Uncle Pugg. And he always gives me presents and says I'm his favorite niece.

He's always lived with us and worked at Daddy's store part time. His lung troubles make him disabled, so he gets a check every month from the government. They think he inhaled so much smoke he'll never recover. The scars are mostly on his body under his clothes so you can't ever see them except on his left wrist and under his left ear. He never talks about it except to Uncle Newton, who was in the war, too. Sometimes his asthma gets so bad he has to sit perfectly still for three or four hours. So he can't get a job anywhere, of course—except helping Daddy out at the store. Daddy says he makes a big difference and is very dependable—unless he's drunk.

I don't know what Mama will do about getting him out of the taxi and up the steps since I'll be living here in Listre. Mary Faye and Norris will have to help. But Mama hates for them to be exposed to such.

Charles *knew* all about Uncle Nate and how I— how my whole family—feels about drinking.

So at the rehearsal Friday night everything was going fine except Mama caught Norris hiding in the baptism place and made him sit on the front row. She'd already caught him once. I told him the water would flow in there and drown him if he didn't watch out. Mary Faye was one of my attendants and being as smart as she could be.

I'm standing in the back of the church with Daddy and Flora, my cousin, who directed the wedding, and I notice that Charles's friend, Buddy Shellar, from Maryland, who I had never met until that night, keeps going outside. And Charles keeps following him. Phil, Jim, Dale, and Crafton—my cousins—were of course staying in their places like they were supposed to. Flora gives me a little push and I start down the aisle with Daddy. Charles is standing with this red-faced grin. When Preacher Gordon says you may kiss the bride, I turned to Charles and there were these little red blood vessels in his left eye that looked like red thread and all of a sudden I caught a whiff of you-know-what. It hit me. It all suddenly fell together. I thought they had been going outside to *talk*.

The thing you won't believe is: Charles's daddy looked lit too.

I did not kiss Charles. I kept my lips clamped. I grabbed him by the arm and led him right up the aisle and out the front door. Madora Bryant, my maid of honor, and some of the other girls were clapping as hard as they could. They couldn't tell what was really happening. When I got him out on the front porch—right beside the bell rope—I said: (now I was really tore up) "Charles, I have told you for months about the condition Uncle Nate has put our family in with alcohol, and you promised me you would not have a bachelor party and get drunk and here you are, drunk, under the nose of Preacher Gordon, Mama, Daddy, Flora and Aunt Naomi and Aunt Flossie and my bridesmaids and Mary Faye and Norris and I will never forget this as long as I live."

"Raney," he says, "first of all, I am not having a bachelor party, and second of all, I am not drunk. I am not doing anybody any harm. I—"

"Not doing any harm? Charles, I—"

"Raney, Buddy drove all the way down here from Baltimore, Maryland, and he has one little pint of something in his car, and we were in the *war* together and if you will just relax. And he's the *only* one of my close friends in the wedding. All these damn cousins of yours."

"Charles, please do not start cussing right here on church property. And if you are mad about my cousins being in the wedding I would have appreciated you saying something about that before now—like while I was spending all my time getting this whole thing planned."

Charles's daddy, Dr. Shepherd, walks up. I could not believe what was happening, yet I dared not make a scene in front of him. I was thinking that if Mama and Aunt Naomi and Aunt Flossie found out about all this drinking I would die.

"Raney, honey," Dr. Shepherd says, "you look adorable." He's a big man and wears those glasses without any rims—shaped like stop signs. He's a math professor, of all things. A doctor. And Mrs. Shepherd is a school teacher. They use these long words I know Mama and Daddy don't know. And they should know Mama and Daddy don't know them. But they'll go on back down to Atlanta after the wedding and we won't see them except maybe a few times a year. Charles says they belong to a country club and all that. What gets me is that Charles said he explained to them about us being Christians and not drinking which I didn't even know we *had* to explain until Madora told me that Charles's parents would probably be used to drinking spiked punch at weddings and what were we going to do?

I hadn't thought about it. I've never been to a wedding where they drink liquor in the punch. I mean there's usually a preacher at a wedding and it's usually at a church. But Madora explained how rich people—or at least Episcopalians and Catholics and sometimes Methodists—will get married in church and then ride over to a country club or someplace where they all drink up a storm.

Dr. Shepherd stands there kind of flushed and glassy-eyed and tells me how proud he is—and he laughs at everything he says, funny or not—

24

and I'll be durn if he didn't reach up right then and there and pull the church bell rope and ring the bell. I could just see old Mrs. Bledsoe, down the road, figure it was not Friday night at all, but Wednesday night—prayer meeting night—instead, and get all upset and maybe grab *Mr.* Bledsoe, who can't hear, and cart him off to a prayer meeting which don't exist. Not to mention all the other people in hearing distance.

The rehearsal dinner was in the education building around behind the church. I walked down the church steps between Charles and his daddy—their arms locked through mine—not able to say a word, and hot behind my ears with embarrassment at the prospect of a scandal.

When we got to the education building there was Mrs. Shepherd—Millie—standing at the door, smiling.

"Smooth as could be," she said, and kissed Dr. Shepherd on the lips—right there in the door to the education building.

Inside, there were two long tables and a head table. Aunt Naomi was in charge. She had got Betty Winnberry to cater. Steaks. T-bone steaks. French fries. The works. I had hoped all along it wouldn't be tacky—like paper tablecloths, which Aunt Naomi was talking about along at first. I'm certainly not going to be cow-tied to any fancy ways of the Shepherds, but I did want things to be proper for everybody concerned.

On the tables were about twelve or thirteen red-checkered, overlapped tablecloths that Aunt Flossie had borrowed from Penny's Grill (and had to wash and dry later that night in order to get them back to the grill in time for Penny to serve breakfast. They open at six A.M.) And over in the corner Mack Lumley was sitting on a bale of hay playing his guitar. He didn't charge but ten dollars, and furnished the hay, too. Somebody suggested me and Charles sing, but I think singing at your own wedding wouldn't be right.

Aunt Flossie had put together the prettiest flower arrangment—right in the middle of the head table: roses, daisies, and Queen Anne's lace, and pittosporum and nandina for greenery.

Just before supper, Charles and Buddy went out for you-know-what, I guess. I had to keep smiling and be as nice as I could to everybody. The supper *was* meaningful, but while I was cutting a piece of T-bone steak I bent over to Charles and whispered: "Charles, I will never forget this." But Charles just turned to Daddy and started talking about the Braves. They always talk about the Braves. As soon as they see one another they start talking about the Braves. I wanted to say, "Daddy, don't you see what Charles is doing? How can you sit there and talk about the Braves while Charles is doing what he's doing?" But I didn't say anything. Lord knows, there was disturbance enough.

I had spent all that time working out the arrangements and Charles wrote all the invitations by hand—he has this beautiful handwriting—and we had talked all about his new library job and our house and our future and how everything was going to work out, and he had been so good about running little errands. Then this.

Charles is very intelligent, and good looking in his own way—his head is slightly large, but I think it just seems that way because his shoulders are narrow—and, oh, we had one or two little fusses getting ready for the wedding, but no more than you'd shake a stick at. And we've been playing music at different gatherings right along through all this—getting better and better and having lots of fun. Charles learns real fast and we like the same music mostly.

Then I end up sitting at my own wedding rehearsal dinner fussing at Charles for doing the one thing I was hoping against hope wouldn't happen ever since Madora explained about how some people get drunk at weddings. We had talked about drinking several times, and I had this feeling of not being able to get a clear picture of how Charles felt. He talks a lot about "psychology."

The actual wedding itself went off without a hitch. It was the most wonderful day of my life. Charles was perfect. Dr. and Mrs. Shepherd were perfect. Mary Faye and Norris were perfect.

27

Mama and Daddy were perfect. Mama wore a long dress—pink—and she was real pretty, except her hair-do was a little tight. Daddy looked the way he always does at church: out of place in a suit, and his head white where his hat goes, and his face red. (He *looks* like he has high blood pressure, but it's normal and always has been.) Right before we walked down the aisle, he said, "Honey, I'm real happy for you. Charles is a good man." His chin was quivering, and two tears rolled down his cheeks. He was holding my hand, which was something I don't remember him doing since I was a little girl. Daddy don't show much emotion.

A bunch of people said it was the nicest wedding they had ever been to. I was just flushed throughout the whole thing. It went exactly according to plans. Charles was handsomer than I've ever seen him. The shoulders in his tux were padded.

The wedding was fairly short and we all went straight to the reception in the education building *without* getting our pictures made, so people wouldn't have to wait. Mama was real worried about us not getting a photographer, but Mack Lumley did it for only ten dollars over cost.

Mama and Mrs. Shepherd—Millie—cried several times each, and so did Flora and Aunt Naomi and Aunt Flossie, and two or three times Dr. Shepherd gave Millie a long hug right in front of everybody. Charles's friend, Buddy Shellar, spent some time talking to Mary Faye and Norris. I thought that was nice. Buddy and my cousins fixed up our car with tin cans and shaving cream; we changed clothes; Sylvia Curtis caught the bouquet; we ran to Charles's Dodge Dart under all that rice, and headed for Myrtle Beach.

Now. The honeymoon. I do not have the nerve to explain everything that happened on the first night there in the Holiday Inn. We had talked about it some before—or Charles had talked about it. And we had, you know, necked the same as any engaged couple. And I had told Charles way back, of course, that I wanted my marriage consumed *after* I was married. Not before. Because if it was consumed before, then I would have to carry the thought of that throughout my entire life and it's hard to undo that which has already been done.

I've read books. I've had talks with my mama. And I've read the Bible. You'd think that would prepare a woman for her wedding night.

It didn't. First of all, Charles had rib-eye steaks rolled into our room on this metal table with drawers which could keep the steaks warm. And there in the middle of the table was a dozen red roses. All that was nice.

But in this silver bucket with ice and a white towel was, of all things, a bottle of champagne.

It was a predicament for me, because on the one hand it was all so wonderful, and Charles had planned it all out like the man is supposed to do—I mean, my dream was being fulfilled. Charles was getting things right. But on the other hand, there in the middle of the table rearing its ugly head, as they say, was a bottle of champagne. I've seen enough bottles of champagne after the World Series on TV (when the ballplayers make fools out of themselves and cuss over the airways) to know one when I see it.

Well, I'm not a prude. Getting drunk at your wedding is one thing, but I can understand a little private celebrating, maybe—as a symbol of something wonderful happening. Something symbolic. So I didn't say anything about the champagne. It's very hard to find fault on your wedding night with a dozen red roses staring you full in the face—even though a still, small voice was warning me.

Charles poured me a glass and I said to myself, Why not just a sip, like medicine, and I tried a sip, but that's all. It tasted like Alka Seltzer with honey in it. I politely refused any more. And didn't think Charles would drink over a glass. (I figured you couldn't buy it except in the bottle, and that's why he got it that way.)

We finished eating and Charles pushed the table, with the dishes, out into the hall. I said excuse me, went into the bathroom, put on my negligee and got ready, you know, and came back out to find Charles standing there in his Fruit of the Loom, drinking champagne out of a plastic cup. It was a terrible scene to remember.

I was planning to do what Mama explained to me: get in the bed and let Charles carry out his duties. And I was thinking that's what Charles would be planning to do. But. He had a different idea which I do not have the nerve to explain. It turned into an argument which finally turned into a sort of Chinese wrestling match with my nerves tore all to pieces. Charles kept saying nothing was in the Bible about what married people could or couldn't do. I finally cried, and Charles said he was sorry. It was awful. I cried again the next morning and Charles said he was sorry again. This may be something I can forgive but I don't think I'll ever forget it. Not for a long time.

On the second day, we didn't say much at breakfast, or after. We went to the beach for a while, ate hot dogs for lunch, and then came back to change clothes. Charles asked the manager about us playing music in the motel lounge that night. (We took our instruments in case we got a chance to play.) When he found out we'd do it free the manager said fine.

So on the second night, rather than going to this country music show like we'd planned, we met the manager in the lounge. Charles wore bluejeans and I wore my blue-checkered blouse, jeans, and cowgirl hat. The manager came in and lit all the candles in these orange candle vases. There were only three or four people there. The only thing I didn't like about it was that they served beer. But the bartender went out of his way to be nice.

We decided to play half an hour and see if we could draw an audience. We started with several banjo pieces and then I sang "This World Is Not My Home" and "I'll Fly Away." I like the way those two songs fit together. It gives me something to talk about when I introduce them. Charles is good about letting me talk about the songs. I have played with people who hog it all.

A crowd gathered, and sure enough they liked the music and clapped and somebody requested "Your Cheating Heart" and Charles tried it. He's been learning it for the last month or so. He forgets words pretty easy. Nobody noticed but he sang the same verse twice. He looked at me and I managed to wink in spite of the fact I was still in turmoil from the night before.

We had told the manager we couldn't play past nine-thirty that night. We told him it was our honeymoon and all. The truth is we only know about two hours worth of songs. But I did want to get back up to our bed and start our marriage in the proper manner. It's something I had been thinking about since I was sixteen or seventeen years old and the night before had *not* worked out at all like I thought it would. It had made me a bundle of nerves and I had discovered something in Charles I didn't know existed—something corroded, and him drinking a whole bottle of champagne brought it out. He still hasn't taken serious my principles about drinking. That first night was a awful experience which I can't bring myself to talk about, but I must say things went better on the second night. I was able to explain to Charles how I was supposed to come out of the bathroom in my negligee, go get in the bed, get under the cover, and then he was supposed to go to the bathroom, come out, come get under the cover, and accomplish what was supposed to be accomplished. It all worked the way it was supposed to, and was wonderful, I must say.

Next morning when I came out of the shower, before we went down for breakfast, Charles was talking on the phone to his other main friend besides Buddy Shellar: Johnny Dobbs, who lives in New Orleans. They were all three in the army together.

"She has a great voice," he was saying. "Raney, get your guitar. Wait a minute, Johnny."

Charles put the phone receiver on the bed, got out his banjo, hit a couple of licks and said to me, "Do 'This World Is Not My Home.' Wait a minute, let me introduce you to Johnny." So he did, over the phone, and Johnny sounded real nice.

"Charles," I whispered, "do you know how much this is costing?"

"I'll pay for it," he said. "I've been telling Johnny about your voice."

So I sang "This World Is Not My Home," and Charles asked Johnny if he could hear it clear over the phone and he said he could and then Charles wanted me to do my chicken song—the one I wrote. Charles thinks it's the funniest thing he's ever heard. It *is* a good song, and since Charles was paying. . . . It goes like this:

> The town council chairman came by
>   late last May.
> Said we're sorry, Mr. Oakley, 'bout
>   what we must say.
> But the airport's expanding, we mean
>   you no harm.
> The new north-south runway's gonna
>   point toward your farm.
>
> My chickens ain't laying; my cow has
>   gone dry,
> 'Cause the airplanes keep flying to the
>   sweet by and by,
> To the lights of the city, to the Hawaiian
>   shore,
> While I rock on my front porch and tend
>   to get poor.

I talked to the governor, and told him
    my desire:
Could you please make them airplanes
    fly a little bit higher.
"My chickens ain't laying," I tried to
    explain.
But my words were going north on a
    south-bound train.

My chickens ain't laying; my cow has
    gone dry,
'Cause the airplanes keep flying to the
    sweet by and by,
To the lights of the city, to the Hawaiian
    shore,
While I rock on my front porch and tend
    to get poor.

I talked to a doctor; he gave me a pill.
I talked to a lawyer; you should have
    seen the bill.
I talked to a librarian; he grinned and
    winked his eye.
And he gave me a little book called,
    "Chickens Can Fly."
(Charles says the book is by B. F.
    Skinner)

I read the little book. Taught my
    chickens to fly,

To aim at the intakes as the jet planes
 flew by.
My chickens are gone now, but the
 answer is found:
My kamakazi chickens closed the new
 runway down.
My kamakazi chickens closed the new
 runway down.

When I finished, Charles said Johnny really liked it. They talked another fifteen minutes before Charles finally hung up.

I hugged Charles and said something about the night before. Charles said we ought to *talk* about our "sexual relationship" sometime, and I said okay, but Lord knows I won't be able to *talk* about it. It's something you're supposed to do in a natural manner, not *talk* about. That's why you don't find it talked about in church and school— or at least you shouldn't: it's not supposed to be talked about. It's something which is supposed to stay in the privacy of your own bedroom.

Next morning when we left, the manager was at the desk and he gave us an envelope with a twenty dollar bill in it. Said it was some of the best entertainment they ever had and would we please come back and that he once worked in a hotel in Reno, and he'd heard some better, but he'd sure heard a lot worse.

3

CHARLES IS IN THE BEDROOM COVERED UP IN the bed. There are eleven broken monogrammed glasses here on the kitchen floor and every window in the house is locked from the inside.

This all started last Saturday afternoon when I called Mama as usual. I try to call her every day. We've always been close and I say those television commercials about calling somebody—reaching out and touching—make sense. Belinda Osborne drives to see her mother every day—forty miles round trip—which I'm not about to do. That is too close. Three times a week is often enough. (Belinda's mother is sick a lot though.)

I'd like to be living closer to home and I know Mama and Daddy were disappointed that we didn't move into the Wilkins house, and I would have, but Charles insisted we live here in Listre because it's close to the college. I finally said okay when he promised he would still go to church with me at home in Bethel.

But: he's been going to church less and less, and we've only been married six weeks. He'll take me to Sunday School and drop me off, still wearing his pajamas under his clothes. He's done it twice. Deacon Brooks said since Charles was Methodist he must think he's too good for Free

Will Baptists. He pretended he was kidding, but I could tell he was serious.

Well, as I said, I called Mama last Saturday afternoon and she told me that she had come by with Aunt Naomi and Aunt Flossie to see us that morning but we were gone. They came on in to use the phone to call Annie Godwin so it wouldn't be long distance. (We don't lock the door normally.) Aunt Naomi went to the kitchen to get a glass of water and accidentally broke one of the monogrammed glasses Cousin Emma gave us for a wedding present. Mama told me all this on the phone. I didn't think twice about it. I figured I'd just pick up another glass next time I'm at the mall. I know where they come from.

Sunday, the very next day, we're eating dinner at home in Bethel with Mama, Daddy, Uncle Nate, Mary Faye, and Norris. Mama fixes at least two meats, five or six vegetables, two kinds of cornbread, biscuits, chow-chow, pickles, pies, and sometimes a cake.

Mama says, "Where did you tell me you all were yesterday morning?" She was getting the cornbread off the stove. She's always the last one to sit down.

"At the mall," I said.

"I like where you moved the couch to," says Mama. "It looks better. We waited for you all fifteen or twenty minutes. I'm sorry Naomi broke that glass," she said.

I hadn't mentioned it to Charles. No reason to. He says—and he was serious: "Why were you all in our house?"

I was mortified in my heart.

"We were just using the phone," says Mama. There was a long silence. It built up and then kept going.

"Pass the turnips, Mary Faye," I said. "I couldn't figure out what was wrong in there so I moved things around until it looked better and sure enough it was the couch. The couch was wrong."

My mama ain't nosy. No more than any decent woman would be about her own flesh and blood.

Listen. I don't have nothing to hide. And Lord knows, Charles don't, except maybe some of his opinions.

We finished eating and set in the den and talked for a while and the subject didn't come up again. Charles always gets fidgety within thirty minutes of when we finish eating. He has no appreciation for just setting and talking. And I don't mean going on and on about politics or something like that; I mean just talking—talking about normal things. So since he gets fidgity, we usually cut our Sunday visits short. "Well, I guess we better get on back," I say, while Charles sits over there looking like he's bored to death. I know Mama notices.

Before we're out of the driveway, Charles says,

"Raney, I think you ought to tell your mama and Aunt Naomi and Aunt Flossie to stay out of our house unless somebody's home."

To stay out of *my* own house.

He couldn't even wait until we were out of the driveway. And all the car windows rolled down.

When we got on down the road, out of hearing distance, I said, "Charles, you don't love Mama and never did."

He pulls the car over beside the PEACHES FOR SALE sign across from Parker's pond. And stares at me.

The whole thing has tore me up. "Charles," I said, and I had to start crying, "you don't have to hide your life from Mama and them. Or me. You didn't have to get all upset today. You could understand if you wanted to. You didn't have to get upset when I opened that oil bill addressed to you, either. There ain't going to be nothing in there but a oil bill, for heaven's sake, Why anyone would want to hide a oil bill I cannot understand."

He starts hollering at me. The first time in my life anybody has set in a car and hollered at me. His blood vessels stood all out. I couldn't control myself. It was awful. If you've ever been hollered at, while you are crying, by the one person you love best in the world, you know what I mean. This was a part of Charles I had never seen.

Here's what happened yesterday. We went to Penny's Grill for lunch. (I refuse to cook three meals a day, I don't care what Mama says.) When we got back, there was Mama's green Ford—parked in front of the house.

"Is that your mother's Ford?" says Charles.

"Where?"

"There."

"Oh, in front of the house? I think it might be." That long silence from the dinner table last Sunday came back, and I hoped Mama was out in the back yard picking up apples because I knew I couldn't stand another scene within a week. I couldn't think of a thing to say. I didn't want to fuss at Charles right before he talked to Mama, and I certainly wouldn't dare fuss at Mama.

Charles got out of the car not saying a word and started for the house. I was about three feet behind, trying to keep up. The front door was wide open.

Charles stopped just inside the door. I looked over his shoulder and there was Mama coming through the arched hall doorway. She stopped. She was dressed for shopping.

"Well, where in the world have you all been?" she says.

"We been to eat," I said.

"Eating out?"

41

"Mrs. Bell," says Charles, "please do not come in this house if we're not here."

I could not believe what I was hearing. It was like a dream.

Mama says, "Charles son, I was only leaving my own daughter a note saying to meet me at the mall at two o'clock, at the fountain. The front door was open. You should lock the front door if you want to keep people out."

"Mrs. Bell, a person is entitled to his own privacy. I'm entitled to my own privacy. This is my—our—house. I—"

"This is my own daughter's house, son. My mama was never refused entrance to my house. She was always welcome. Every day of her life."

I was afraid Mama was going to cry. I opened my mouth but nothing came out.

"Mrs. Bell," says Charles, "it seems as though you think everything *you* think is right, is right for everybody."

"Charles," I said, "that's what everybody thinks—in a sense. That's even what *you* think."

Charles turned half around so he could see me. He looked at me, then at Mama.

Mama says, "Son, I'll be happy to buy you a new monogrammed glass if that's what you're so upset about. Naomi didn't mean to break that glass. I'm going over to the mall right now. And I know where they come from."

Charles walks past me and out the front door, stops, turns around and says, "I didn't want any of those damned monogrammed glasses in the first place and I did the best I could to make that clear, plus that's not the subject." (I gave him a monogrammed blue blazer for his birthday and he cut the initials off before he'd wear it.)

So now Mama's at the mall with her feelings hurt. Charles is in the bedroom with a blanket over his head, and I'm sitting here amongst eleven broken monogrammed glasses, and every door and window locked from the inside.

Evidently Charles throws things when he's very mad. I never expected violence from Charles Shepherd. Thank God we don't have a child to see such behavior.

We didn't speak all afternoon, or at supper—I fixed hot dogs, split, with cheese and bacon stuck in—or after. I went to bed about ten o'clock, while Charles sat in the living room reading some book. I felt terrible about Mama's feelings being hurt like I know they were; I hadn't known whether to call her or not; I couldn't with Charles there; and I couldn't imagine what had got into Charles.

I went to bed and was trying to go to sleep, with my mind full of upsetting images, when I heard this *voice* coming out of the heating vent at the head of the bed on my side. I sat up. I thought at first it was somebody under the house. I let my head lean down over the side of the bed close to the vent. It was *Charles*—talking on the phone in the kitchen.

Now if we'd been on speaking terms I would have told him I could hear him, but we weren't speaking. And besides, I won't about to get out of bed for no reason at eleven P.M. And so I didn't have no choice but to listen, whether I wanted to or not.

Charles was talking to his Johnny friend. I could hear just about everything he said. If we had been speaking, I wouldn't have hesitated to tell him how the sound came through the vent. But we weren't speaking, as I said. He was talking about—you guessed it: Mama.

". . . She just broke in, in essence . . . just walked through the door when nobody was home. . . . It's weird, Johnny. . . . What am I supposed to do?"

Now why didn't he ask *me* what he was supposed to do? He didn't marry Johnny Dobbs.

I agree that some things need to be left private—but the *living room?* The living room is where everybody comes into the house. That's one of the last places to keep private on earth. I just can't connect up Charles's idea about privacy to the living room.

He went on about Mama for a while and then said something about everybody saying "nigger," and that when Johnny came to see us for him not to drive in after dark—which I didn't understand until it dawned on me that maybe Johnny Dobbs was a, you know, black. He didn't sound like it when I talked to him over the phone at Myrtle Beach. Charles and his other army buddy, Buddy Shellar, at the wedding kept talking about "Johnny this" and "Johnny that" but I never thought about Johnny being anything other than a regular white person. They were all three in the army, which of course everybody knows has been segregated since 1948, according to Charles, so I guess it's possible they roomed together, or at least ate together.

He didn't sound, you know, black.

I'll ask Charles about it when we're on speaking terms and I'll tell him about how the sound comes through the vent; but if he is a nigger, he can't stay here. It won't work. The Ramada, maybe, but not here.

4

AUNT FLOSSIE CALLED LAST WEDNESDAY— said to come by and pick up some fresh peanut butter cookies. She lives in a little four-room house between Listre and Bethel—and cooks apple pies for Penny's Grill on the side. Her kitchen is always smelling like cinnamon and sugar-cooked apples. Charles can't get over how

45

good her apple pies are. He asked her for the recipe and he don't even cook.

"I'm cooking an extra apple pie," she says. "I'll be done in a few minutes and you can have a hot piece with some ice cream." Aunt Flossie has a way about her that makes me feel free to talk. She seems like she's used to talking, even though she lives by herself. When something hard to talk about comes up, there's a little sparkle in her eyes—and she loves to tell stories almost as much as Uncle Nate. I went right over there.

"You know," she said, "when Frank and me got married it was like starting to school—the things I had to learn. I guess I'd never had an argument with a soul in the world—except a few squabbles with Mama." She was making up cookie dough. (Now, how could she tell that Charles and me had had a argument?) "I don't know about Frank," she said, "but I don't guess he'd ever argued with a woman, certainly not his mama. We had to *learn* to argue. I'd get so mad at him. We'd stay mad for days, not speaking. I finally figured out that that kind of business scared me. Scared me bad. And that's why I was so mad. Like with old man Wiley's bull, Red—us being scared and mad getting run together at the same time."

"Old man Wiley's bull?"

"I shot old man Wiley's bull one time. Named

Red. I couldn't have been over twelve. He was always getting loose and chasing us up a tree. Mama told Mr. Wiley to keep his bull locked up, else she'd shoot him. Course I heard all this talk—so one day all of us were down in the woods when Red got out and started pawing dirt, throwing his head around, and snorting, and I ran to the house and snuck the shotgun out the back door. Everybody was up a tree when I got back. I shot him. He turned and run and I shot him again. We hated that bull. And the reason we hated him was we were so scared of him. Why, the bull won't doing nothing unnatural. And the whole point is, we were mad *because* we were scared and I never figured *that* out until me and Frank figured out about our arguments."

"Whose bull was it?"

"It was old man Wiley's bull. One day I told Frank that our arguments scared me and—"

"What happened to the bull?"

"Oh, he won't hurt none. The gun had birdshot. Ah, the pies are ready."

There's no apple pie in the world better than Aunt Flossie's, especially with cold vanilla ice cream melting down over it.

Uncle Frank died when I was about seven. He was a car salesman. I don't remember much about him. But I've seen lots of pictures of him and Aunt Flossie, Mama and Daddy, and Aunt Naomi and Uncle Forrest, who died sometime before I was six. They all went to the beach, the fair, and the mountains together and took bunches of pictures.

"How old was I when Uncle Forrest died?"

"Four. Three or four, I guess. Frank used to call him 'Woody.' What a card he was. Always kidding. People always liked that about him though. I never saw him embarrassed but once. Did I ever tell you about the time we all went to the beach before him and Naomi were married?"

"I don't think so."

"Well, me and Doris were swimming in the ocean when here comes Naomi and Forrest from the bath house. They don't get no farther than about a foot deep—where the waves are breaking for the third or fourth time—and Naomi is holding onto Forrest's hand and jumping every little wave and screaming like nobody's business when Doris—who's standing behind me—says, 'Lord have mercy.' I look and there's Naomi just jumping up and down over those little waves, laughing, and one of her breasts—just as white as flour—was out of her bathing suit and Forrest—they weren't married yet—was looking off down the beach, like he hadn't noticed. Doris says, 'Lord have mercy, Flossie, one of Naomi's dinners has fell out.' Well, I thought I would die. I started walking toward them, motioning to Naomi, and she just kept jumping up and down. Forrest was pretending he hadn't noticed—

looking off down the beach. Naomi saw and turned away from Forrest and bent over double and got everything tucked back in. Forrest was standing there embarrassed to death and I said, 'Tell us a joke, Woody.' But the funniest thing was your mama saying, 'One of Naomi's dinners has fell out.' "

A pan of cookies was done—and Aunt Flossie wrapped me up a bunch in wax paper and put them in a cookie can.

"Anyway, honey, try not to worry too much about the rough spots."

"What rough spots?"

"With Charles—if and when."

"Oh, there ain't no rough spots." I couldn't get into all that about Charles. Even with Aunt Flossie. If it got worse: maybe.

"I mean any you might have."

"Oh. Well, Charles is just as sweet as he can be. We been working up some new music. We learned three new Carter family tunes last week. I'll let you know if there get to be any rough spots."

"You be sure to do that," says Aunt Flossie. "It never hurts to have somebody to listen."

A week or two ago, Charles said he wished he had a Aunt Flossie in his family. His aunts are all out West, or in Connecticut.

5

AUNT NAOMI CALLED ME THIS PAST Wednesday was a week ago and upset me terrible. She called to find out all about our upcoming trip to the beach: when, exactly, we were coming back, what food she needed to take, and so forth. She also said Mama was upset about the argument with Charles—they had talked about it on the phone—but that Mama wouldn't say nothing to me about it for the world. She said Mama felt betrayed and couldn't understand why it all had to happen to her.

Well, it just made me sick. I don't know why Charles had to react so. Mama would never hurt anything in the world, and Charles knows it.

Now Aunt Naomi, as well as Mama, has got something against Charles. The problem is that nobody has seen the good side of anybody else—in the whole family, since the wedding—except, I guess Daddy has pretty much seen the good side of Charles, and has took to Charles better than anybody else. Except me, of course—and maybe Aunt Flossie.

So anyway, when we drove to the beach last Sunday (we left right after Sunday School), Charles insisted on sitting up front with Daddy, so they could talk about surf fishing. They had these great long fishing rods, and some short ones, tied to the top of the car. I don't know why they don't just use the short ones, which are way less expensive, and fish off the pier like other people. They can get their line farther out in the ocean that way. Those big rods cost a fortune.

I wanted Charles to sit in the back with me and Aunt Naomi so they could get to know each other's good sides a little better, and so Mama and Daddy could sit up front where they could argue by themselves. But oh no. Charles gets up front before anybody else has a chance. Me, Mama, and Aunt Naomi sat in the back. Uncle Nate, Aunt Flossie, Mary Faye, and Norris followed us in Aunt Flossie's Oldsmobile.

The funny thing is this: Charles has not gone anywhere with Daddy driving—and Daddy don't always chew tobacco when he drives but last Sunday he did; and what he does when he chews tobacco and drives is use a drink bottle, usually a short Coke-a-cola bottle, for a spitoon. When I saw Daddy bringing a Coke bottle to the car I figured it served Charles right for not wanting to ride in the back with Aunt Naomi.

See, Charles has a repulsion about anything gooey and slimey. He won't eat boiled okra and he thinks somebody spitting is just awful, whereas I don't see nothing wrong with it as long as it's not on somebody.

Sometimes if Daddy takes a chew while he's driving, and a Coke bottle's not around, he'll open the car door at a stop sign and spit on the road—which might have been better for Charles on this trip—but when he does that, the tobacco spatters up, and the car door gets to looking like a speckled dog until Mama goes out and cleans it off with Ajax.

So Sunday, as soon as Daddy gets settled behind the steering wheel, he cuts off this big hunk of Brown Williamson. I buy him four plugs every Christmas and I buy Mama a bottle of Jergen's lotion. Of course that's not all I buy. Last Christmas I bought Daddy a pair of ceramic bird dogs and I bought Mama a off-white shawl which she took back. She takes back most things she buys or you give her. She's always hard to buy for. She'll *tell* you she's hard to buy for. One Christmas, Ferbie Layton told Aunt Flossie that Mama was pretty and Aunt Flossie told me and Aunt Naomi that she was passing along the compliment to Mama as a Christmas present because for sure Mama couldn't return that. If she does keep something you give her, she'll alter it. One Christmas I gave her a free-hanging plaid blouse which she said she believed she'd take up even though we all told her it was the right length. So she finally said she wouldn't take it up. Aunt Flossie said she bet she would. (I think she did, but we never knew for sure.)

We hadn't got as far as Paulsen's Gulf when Daddy pulls his Coke bottle up from between his legs and spits in a long string of brown juice. He breaks the spit off by flicking the mouth of the Coke bottle against his bottom lip. Comes clear every time.

Charles squirmed. I wanted to say Charles if you weren't watching out for yourself so much, you wouldn't have to be up there; you could be back here in the back seat getting to know Aunt Naomi a little better, and Mama could be up front with Daddy so they wouldn't have to argue back and forth across the seat.

Then Mama says what she always says at the Oak Hill intersection when we go to the beach: "Thurman, you're going to turn to the right here?"

"Yes I am, Doris."

"You're not going by the interstate?"

"Doris, I'll be glad to let you drive if you want to."

"I just asked, Thurman. Remember we clocked it."

"I remember we clocked it."

"Well, it was longer when we went this way."

"That was early of a Friday morning when the traffic was thick."

"Thurman, the point is you don't have all them little towns to drive through on the interstate."

"Doris, I'll be glad to let you drive if you want to."

"Well, I'm just thinking of how not to take so

long to get there. I declare," says Mama to Aunt Naomi, "the 'blacks' stop in these little towns in the middle of the street and talk to whoever happens to be on the sidewalk and you can't blow your horn lest one's liable to come back for all you know and cut your throat." (Mama has started saying "blacks" when Charles is around. And I guess I have too.)

"I'll be glad to let you drive if you want to," Daddy says.

"Okay."

"What?"

"Okay, I'll drive," says Mama.

There was a long pause during which the car didn't slow down a bit.

"I'll drive," says Daddy.

"Well then," says Mama, "you shouldn't say you'll be glad for me to drive." There was this other long pause. "When you're not."

Daddy just looked at Charles, shifted his tobacco from one cheek to the other and says, "You got any connector sleeves in your tackle box? I'm out."

Charles said he had plenty.

For the past ten years, every time we go to the beach, we eat at Hardee's in Goldsboro. So when we got close, Daddy says, "Ya'll want to eat at Hardee's?"

"Any place is fine with me," says Mama.

And do you know what Charles has the gall to say? He says, "I'd rather eat at some place we can sit down to order, if it's all the same."

I could not believe my ears.

One reason Charles had to speak up is because he took a course at the college called Aggressiveness Training. It teaches you to say what you want to say when you want to say it. The thing is: Charles never needed any aggressiveness training. He's never had any problem being aggressive. But he thinks it's the modern way or something.

"I want to eat at Hardee's so I can get a apple turnover," I said.

Daddy said he didn't care, someplace to sit down and order would be fine with him, but Mama and Aunt Naomi sided with me.

You see, Charles tries out his aggressiveness training when in his heart he really don't care. He just wants to keep it in practice—keep it working, like when you break up a flower bed in winter just to keep it loose.

We ate at Hardee's.

After lunch, me and Charles traded car seats. His idea.

Now. You would think Charles could ride to the beach without disagreeing with Aunt Naomi right there in the back seat. But oh no. It was over a very simple matter.

Aunt Naomi goes to our church but she lives

out in the country, close to Hillview Baptist—not a Free Will, and while we rode along she told all about them having to let their preacher go.

"After it all got out they didn't have no choice but to let him go," says Aunt Naomi. "They say it started out with him praying regular with this woman whose husband got killed in a car wreck. I didn't know her—or her husband. She hadn't been around long. I think they were praying every Wednesday night after prayer meeting. She up and moves to Charlotte and nobody thought anything about it until Tim Hodges, who's the treasurer, noticed these regular phone calls on the church phone bill. One was over thirty minutes. He told Lloyd Womble, the head deacon. I guess they kept a eye on things and one Friday after the preacher said he was going to see his brother in Franklin, they checked up on him. Called his brother. His brother hadn't seen him and won't expecting him. Well.

"Saturday, when the preacher got back, Tim and Lloyd paid him a visit. Asked him where he'd been and he said to see his brother. And of course they had him. Just plain had him."

"They certainly are a trusting bunch," says Charles.

"Well, yes," says Aunt Naomi, "they trust in the Lord, of course." She was looking straight at the back of Charles's head. "Now the funny part was that Emily, the preacher's wife, didn't get

56

mad at the preacher—that I know of. She got mad at Tim and Lloyd because they wouldn't believe it when the preacher said he was sorry. She said *she* believed he was sorry. But what else would the man say—caught red-handed. Tim and Lloyd felt obliged to bring it before the church and the church voted him out. He had to move."

After a minute, Charles says, "It's possible that Jesus would have forgiven him. After all, he forgave a prostitute."

That took the cake. I've been going to church since I was born and I don't remember anything about Jesus forgiving a prostitute.

Besides that, a prostitute is not married like the preacher was.

Aunt Naomi just looked out the window, then hunted through her pocketbook for some chewing gum and said, "Well, I don't know about that."

We stay at Mr. Albert Douglas's cabin at the beach every summer. He rents it to us at half price and it's only two blocks from the ocean. We found the key on the nail in the stumpy tree beside the back door and let ourselves in. Everything had been left in order. We opened all the windows to get rid of the closed-in smell. There was a nice breeze.

Uncle Nate took Norris and Mary Faye for a quick look at the ocean while the rest of us unpacked. I insisted me and Charles get the couch to sleep on since we'd probably be staying up later than anybody else.

We had barely got settled when Uncle Nate's asthma started acting up. It usually does at the beach. He sat down on the couch and said he'd sit there for a spell. He was breathing fast, pulling back with his shoulders on each breath, and giving a little wheezy cough every minute or so. His hair was slicked straight back with Vitalis and he was wearing a starched white shirt as usual.

Norris and Mary Faye came in begging Charles and me to take them to the boardwalk. I kind of wanted to go to the boardwalk myself. I like the hubbub. So Charles and me took them. We all got a ice cream cone as soon as we got there, but before Norris took the first bite, his scoop fell out. Vanilla—he won't eat nothing but vanilla. He started to pick it up.

"Stupid," said Mary Faye.

"Norris," I said, "ask the lady for another scoop. Don't pick that up off the boardwalk." He already had most of it up. He let it drop back. The lady saw what happened and had him another scoop ready when he reached up his cone. I got some napkins and wiped off his hand.

We walked along the boardwalk. I looked back to check on Norris. He was walking along, looking back over his shoulder at this little boy with a stuffed giraffe. His ice cream cone was tilting more and more.

"Norris, don't drop your—"

That scoop fell between the planks and left just the slightest bit up top. Norris squatted down and looked.

The lady made us pay this time. I guess she was worried about going out of business.

Charles bought me a necklace from one of those little jewelry stands. I told him it was too expensive but he bought it anyway and had "Love, Tiger" wrote on it. He does little things like that, that a lot of men never think about. I tried to get him to ring the bell with the sledge hammer, but he wouldn't. Norris wanted to but I wouldn't let him. He would have been disappointed. I did let him and Mary Faye ride the bumper cars three times. They got the bottoms of their feet so black Aunt Naomi made them wash them off with soap at the outside shower before she'd let them come in the cottage.

We had pimento cheese and monkey meat— that's luncheon meat—sandwiches and potato chips for supper. Then after supper while Daddy was unfolding the card table for Rook, Aunt Naomi wanted to know how thick the niggers had been down at the boardwalk.

"Not very," I said. "They hang out mostly over

at Wright's beach." That's the nigger beach. "I don't think I saw over one or two."

"I saw a whole car load," says Norris.

"They've got as much right as anyone else to walk on the boardwalk," says Charles. Charles has this thing about niggers. For some reason he don't understand how they are. Or at least how they are around Listre and Bethel. Maybe his Johnny friend is different. I can only speak for the ones around Listre and Bethel.

"Well, son," says Aunt Naomi, "I agree they got a right. The Constitution gives them a right. So that's settled. There's no question about that. No argument at all about that. The problem comes with where they want to spend their time. And so long as they've got *their* beach, like Raney says, then I don't understand to my life why they don't use it—why they have to use ours. In Russia they wouldn't have their own beach. But our constitution does provide that they can have their own beach. I agree. It's just that they need to stay in their own place at their own beach just like the white people stay at their own place at their own beach."

Nobody else said anything—Uncle Nate was asleep on the couch—but you could tell we all agreed except Charles. He walks through the screen door on outside.

"I don't understand where he gets some of his attitudes," says Aunt Naomi. "What's trumps?"

· · ·

Monday morning, Mama and me cooked eggs, bacon, grits, and biscuits. After breakfast, Daddy, Uncle Nate, and Charles took Mary Faye and Norris fishing at the pier. Me, Mama, Aunt Naomi, and Aunt Flossie cleaned up the dishes, put on our bathing suits, got towels and suntan lotion, and walked to the beach. We were all planning to meet back at the cabin for lunch.

About the time we got settled on a nice even spot, along came this Marine with a woman who had a blue lightning bolt tattooed on the inside of her knee. They sat down on this white towel— too little for both of them— beside some college students. The waves were crashing, so I know they couldn't hear us talk.

"I declare I don't think I've ever seen a woman with a tatoo," says Mama.

"Where?" says Aunt Naomi.

"On the inside of her knee."

"No, *where?* Where are they?"

"Oh. Right over there."

"He looks like a soldier."

"He's a Marine from Camp Lejune," I said. "I can tell by the way his hair's cut."

"I don't see no tattoo on her," says Aunt Naomi.

"Wait a minute and you will," says Mama.

"There it is," says Aunt Flossie.

"Well, I'll be dog," says Aunt Naomi. "Don't

that beat all? A blue lightning bolt. Do you reckon she drew that on there with a ball point pen?"

"Not unless she can draw mighty good," says Mama. "Course a lightning bolt ain't all that hard to draw. I remember from school."

"Now can you imagine," says Aunt Naomi, "some woman walking into a tattoo parlor with a bunch of men standing around, hiking up her dress and saying I want a blue lightning bolt tattooed right here on the inside of my knee? Can you imagine that?"

"Well, I sure can't," says Mama. "But she looks like she's been in plenty places like that. I mean she looks like she's spent a good deal of her life indoors in some back room."

"Well, she could be a you-know-what," says Aunt Naomi.

The woman was pale and skinny with black hair stringy wet from swimming. She lit a cigarette and when she pulled it out of her mouth she laughed smoke at something the Marine said and I could see some of her teeth were rotten.

"Young people nowadays will go to almost any length," said Aunt Naomi. "I don't know what it's all coming to. Who ever heard of so much burning, beating, and stabbing, and my Lord, I can't imagine what Papa would done to me had I come home with a blue lightning bolt tattooed on my kneecap. Why he would—"

"It's on the inside of her knee," says Mama.

"Why he would have skint me alive."

Up walked Charles all of a sudden and said we'd better come to the house, that Norris had a fish hook hung in his *nose*. He said that on Mary Faye's first cast, Norris was walking behind her and the hook caught him, as clean as day, in his left nostril—with *the worm still on the hook*. We followed him to the cottage. I couldn't imagine.

We walk in and there sits Norris in a straightback chair, crying, with Uncle Nate down on his knees trying to see in Norris's nose and Norris trying to hold his head still but not being able to on account of crying.

Norris rolls his eyes to look at us when we walk in. Standing there beside him is Mary Faye, holding a rod and Zebco reel with a line leading to Norris's nose where the hook is stuck in his nostril with a live worm half in and half out. It won't bleeding though. Daddy is standing behind Uncle Nate, watching.

"I say we ought to take him to the hospital," says Charles.

"Wait a minute," says Uncle Nate, "if the barb ain't in we can pull it right out."

"If the barb ain't in, it would've fell out, wouldn't it?—with that great big worm on there," says Aunt Flossie. "He must weigh half a pound."

"You don't need that much worm to catch a fish," says Aunt Naomi.

"I think we ought to take him to the hospital," says Charles.

"I agree," I said. In many ways Charles is very clearheaded.

"Well, if I can just—" said Uncle Nate, reaching up toward Norris's nose.

Norris lets out this short yell and puts his hand in front of his face.

Uncle Nate stands up and looks around at everybody.

"Take him to the hospital," says Charles.

"I don't think so," says Uncle Nate.

Tears are dropping off the worm. A drop of blood appears.

"It's bleeding," says Charles. "What's wrong with taking him to the hospital?"

"That's the worm bleeding," says Uncle Nate.

"How do you know that?" asks Charles.

"Cause it's a blood worm. They're supposed to bleed. That's what it's called: a blood worm. That's what it says where you buy them on the pier: blood worms, $2.00 a dozen."

"Gosh, they've gone up," says Aunt Naomi.

"Well, suppose it is the worm," says Charles. "What can you lose by taking him to the hospital?"

"The worm or Norris?" says Mary Faye.

"Norris," says Charles.

"If Norris goes, the worm goes," says Aunt Naomi.

"To start with," says Uncle Nate to Charles, "you're going to lose about fifty dollars. Second, you're going to lose a chance to do something for yourself instead of some overpaid doctor doing it."

Charles walked out the door. Again.

Then Daddy took over. "Now, wait a minute," he said. "Everybody sit down. No. No, not you, Mary Faye. You stand right there and hold the pole, honey." He pulled a chair in front of Norris's chair and sat down. "You all go on about your business. I want to talk to Norris a few minutes. Let me have the rod and reel, Mary Faye. Now, Mr. Norris. I'll bet that nose hurts, don't it?"

Norris nodded his head.

"Why don't you stand up real easy."

Norris stood up, stretching his neck out and holding his head still like a dog smelling a dead snake, his hands hanging down by his sides with his fingers spread like he was afraid of touching something gooey—or like he *had* touched something gooey.

"Okay," said Daddy, "I'll tell you what let's do—do you want to get that old worm out of there?"

Norris nodded his head up and down, easy.

"Now the first thing I want you to do is give me your hand."

Norris reached out his hand and Daddy took it

in his hand and massaged it around and around. "Now you just relax. We'll get that old worm right out of there in no time flat. You think about that little sting as a mosquito bite."

Norris nodded his head up and down. A tear dropped.

"Now you take holt of the line right here— that's right. Right there. That's good. Now you just move your hand up along the line until it gets up to that little hook. Okay. Now. You relax and I'm going to wrap my hand around your hand and help you out a little bit."

Norris nodded up and down, slow. His eyes were getting bigger.

"Hold your head real still and we'll—"

Daddy nudged up and then down, and that hook came right out—as pretty as you please. Aunt Flossie went over and hugged Norris and he started bawling and his nose started bleeding but we put some cold towels on it. Mama got a little alcohol on some cotton up in there and then some Vaseline. Norris cried with the alcohol but calmed down with the Vaseline.

We ate banana sandwiches for lunch. Then me and Uncle Nate went along with Daddy and Charles to watch them surf fish. First we stopped by the fish market and bought some fish to cut up and use for bait; then we drove to this spot where Daddy said the blues might be biting.

They'd cast far out with a piece of dead fish on the hook, then stand there for ten or fifteen minutes before winding in the line to check the bait, which was smoothed down and considerably smaller than when they first threw it out. Charles said the sand and current did that. He let me hold his rod for a while, then he asked Uncle Nate if he wanted to hold it for a while, but he said no, and at about three o'clock Uncle Nate left—said he was going to walk up to the boardwalk and try to find a newspaper. We fished until about five and caught one fish. Daddy caught him but he was too little to keep.

When we got back to the cottage, Mama and the others had been swimming. Everybody was sunburned except Daddy. He wears all his clothes at the beach, all the time, every time we go.

Uncle Nate didn't turn up for supper and I could tell Mama was worried. We had cold fried chicken left over from the trip down, tomatoes, hot snap beans, and fresh hot biscuits, and had finished and been sitting around talking for a while when in walked Uncle Nate: drunk. But I didn't think he was terribly drunk because he looked decent, except he had one sleeve rolled up and the other rolled down and unbuttoned.

"Nate," Mama says, "what in the world have you gone and done?"

"Nothing, Doris, nothing in the worl' but been fishing."

"I declare," says Mama, "you'd think you could come to the beach with your own family and behave yourself."

Daddy walked out on the porch with his oatmeal cookie.

Charles was over on the couch reading a *Time* magazine. Uncle Nate went over and sat down beside him.

"Where'd you go to school, boy?"

"Atlanta."

"They teach you the stays and capols?"

"The what?"

"The stays and capols."

"No, I don't think so."

"You don't think so? You don't think so? Wha's capol of Missesota?" He was drunker than he looked.

"Missesota?" said Charles.

"Minnesota."

"I don't know."

"*You don't know! You don't know! St. Paul.* Hell no, they di'n teach you no capols." Uncle Nate looked around.

"Nate," says Mama, "there'll be no cussing in this beach cottage. You have done enough damage getting drunk in front of these children. It's bad enough without you cussing in the very cottage Al Douglas has been nice enough to rent us at half price."

Uncle Nate looked at her and then turned back

68

to Charles. "Montgomery Alabama, Phoenix Arizona, Little Rock Arkansas, Sacramento California, Denver Colorado. Hell, I know 'em every one."

"Nate," Mama says, "now I have told you—"

"Name a stay," Uncle Nate says to Charles.

"Florida."

"Tallahassee. Ha. See? Capol T-a-l-l-a-h-a-s-s-e-e. We had to learn to spell them too. How come you din have to learn the stays and capols?"

"What good is it?" asks Charles, pushing up off the couch with his hands and slipping away.

"What *good* is it? What *good* is it? Why, hell, if you're traveling through Miss'ippi and somebody says 'what's the capol of this stay?' you say 'St. Paul.' You know something about the stay you're in. What *good* is it? What *good* is it? Hell, why come you learn anything?"

"Nate," says Mama.

"Well," says Charles, "I'm just thinking why not write it all down on a piece of paper, put it in your billfold, and then spend all that time learning something else. Then when somebody wants to know a capital, pull out the piece of paper and read the answer."

"*Read* the answer. *Read* the answer. Shit, when I went to school—"

"Nate!" Mama says. "I said I was not going to have it and I mean it. If you want me to call the law you just keep it up. I'll do it. I'll do it right this very night."

Uncle Nate got quiet, almost whispering—"When I went to school you learned your lessons. You went home and learned your lessons. And when it was time to work you worked. And when it was time to go to church, you went to church. And when it was time to go to bed, you went to bed. And when it was ti—"

"Well, I'm just glad I didn't have to learn the states and capitals," said Charles.

"We had to *spell* them too." Uncle Nate spit on "spell." "Miss'ippi. Capol M-i-s-s-i-s-s-i-p-p-i. Jackson. Capol J-a-c-k-s-o-n."

"Well, I'm glad you learned all that," said Charles, getting up from the couch. "I think it's about time I turned in."

"I don't care if you're too good to talk to me," says Uncle Nate.

"I don't think I'm too good to talk to you."

"Oh yes you do."

"I do not."

"Oh yes, yes, yes you do. I know when somebody thinks they're too good to talk to me. But don't worry, you're not the first one. You just go right ahead off to beddy bye, sonny."

Charles looked at me and I remembered we were sleeping on the couch. Everybody but Daddy had been sitting around listening. They started getting up—except Mama, who was sitting on a stool by the sink—and heading off to bed. It was time anyway. Charles asked me if I wanted to go out and get a breath of fresh air and I said I did.

"I thought you wanted to go to bed?" said Uncle Nate.

"You're sitting on my bed," said Charles.

"I'm sitting on the goddamn couch."

Mama stood up. "Uncle Nate," I said. "Now, listen, Charles does not think he's too good for you. You've just had too much to drink, and I think you ought to cut out that language. You're here with the entire family and the least you can do is be polite. Charles does not think he's too good for you. He's just got his own opinions like anybody else, that's all."

Uncle Nate looked straight at me, with his mouth open and his eyes red and droopy, "You're right, honey," he says. "You're exactly right." And he starts crying. "I love you all more than anything," he says, "and I pray for ever'one of you ever'night. I pray for you, Doris, and you, Raney, and for you, Naomi, and Thurman, and you, Flossie, and the kids and you too, Charles."

"Nate, you'd better pray for yourself," says Mama.

Uncle Nate looked at Mama. His head was bobbing around and tears were on his cheeks. His head got still and he smiled and said, "Oh, I do that first."

"Let's go outside," Charles says to me. I walked over and patted Uncle Nate on the back and then me and Charles went outside while Mama fussed at Uncle Nate for taking the Lord's name in vain.

We walked down to the beach and started toward the pier. Mary Faye was following us. We stopped and she stopped.

"You'll have to go back, Mary Faye," I said.

"Why?"

"You just will."

"I don't want to."

"We're going to walk down to the pier and it's time for you to go to bed."

"I'm not sleepy. Come on. Let me go. Daddy said I could."

I told Charles to wait and I went back and talked to Mary Faye. I figured she might be upset too. I told her that Uncle Nate was a good man at heart and not to be afraid of him, that God moves in mysterious ways, and that Uncle Nate's cussing was the work of the Devil.

She said she just wanted to go to the pier.

So I explained that Charles was upset about Uncle Nate and that I needed to talk to him and that we'd go to the pier tomorrow.

She kicked the sand, making it squeak, turned around and went on back.

At the pier, Charles said Uncle Nate was a "weird bird."

"What do you mean?" I said.

"When he's sober he's so neat, and so infernally obsessive. Drinking water at the same time every day?"

"When he's sober he does. Three o'clock in the afternoon."

"It's just . . . the way he sits around and falls asleep; and then those incredible binges. He's obviously depressed."

"Charles, he had some terrible times in World War II and sometimes he can't hardly breathe with that asthma and emphysema or whatever. He never recovered from the war and Mama's had to take care of him, don't you see? And he won't talk to anybody about what happened to him, except Uncle Newton—all night one night, they say. And Uncle Newton's getting too sick for anybody to talk to, much. And he has to take those drugs for his nerves and his asthma. And he got that terrible burn on over fifty percent of his body. He's got one big awful scar all over his body that he'll have to carry with him all his life, plus his lungs from inhaling all that smoke."

"Raney, there are lots of men who were wounded and had terrible times in World War II, and Vietnam, and World War I. They don't necessarily sit around falling asleep all the time."

"Maybe they sleep at night, Charles. Maybe you don't know all about what's wrong with everybody, and maybe it's something besides 'psychology.' I think part of the problem is you don't think Uncle Nate likes you all that much."

"That's right. And where do you suppose I got that idea? He is obviously jealous. It's not a great deal of fun being around that."

"He's not the only other one in my family who you get to be around, Charles."

"No, he's not the only other one; that's for sure."

"What do you mean by that?"

"Nothing."

It's too bad Charles was a only child brought up without any family around. When he went to see a aunt or uncle, his mama and daddy had to carry him to another state. He just don't have a single sense about family, about having family.

When Uncle Nate is sober he's as nice as he can be. And you'll never find anybody neater. His clothes are always pressed and starched. Well, Mama keeps them that way, but he keeps everything hung up and straight and folded. Then he'll get drunk and filthy and come home and cuss something awful. And nobody able to do a thing unless it's the law. Dorcus Kerr, the deputy sheriff, can usually handle him pretty well. Mama hates it when it comes to that. Daddy usually calls Dorcus, and Dorcus comes in his uniform. He puts it on if he's off duty. Uncle Nate respects a uniform.

By Friday night, Uncle Nate had gotten sober on his own, thank goodness. After supper he wanted to hear "Give Me the Roses," so Charles and me got out our instruments and did it. It's one of our favorites too. It goes like this:

> Wonderful things of folks are said
> When they are passed away.
> Roses adorn their narrow bed
> Over the sleeping clay.
>
> Give me the roses while I live,
> Trying to cheer me on.
> Useless are flowers that you give
> After the soul is gone.

And it has a couple more verses.

Then Daddy wanted to hear "Unclouded Day," which Charles has been wanting to learn ever since I met him. We learned it about three weeks ago. So we did that, and then "Are You Tired of Me, My Darling?" and "Fifty Miles of Elbow Room," two other Carter family tunes Daddy and Charles like. We tried to get everybody to sing on "Fifty Miles," but Uncle Nate and Daddy would be so far off key everybody would start laughing and that would get me laughing and that would get Charles laughing.

When we finished singing, Uncle Nate told

about the Christmas Uncle Pugg went to Raleigh to sell wreaths and holly and mistletoe and got lost and was too proud to ask anybody the way home. He slept that night in a church and the next morning the preacher saw him come out and asked him if he was the man who'd come to fix the steps. Uncle Pugg said he was. He had his tools in a box in the wagon. He fixed the steps and the preacher asked him to fix the roof and so he did that. Then the preacher asked him if he brought the window to put in. Uncle Pugg said he didn't but that a man over in Bethel had the window and could the preacher tell him how to get there. The preacher told him, and Uncle Pugg came on home.

At about ten o'clock when everybody else was going to bed, me and Charles walked out to the pier. Charles said he wasn't even sure about the *names* of anybody in his family, besides his mama and daddy and aunts and uncles. I couldn't imagine aunts and uncles not sitting around and telling all about *their* aunts and uncles.

Out on the pier the breeze was steady and cool and the air had that fresh salty smell without the dead fish smell. The moon was coming up over the water, and waves hit against the poles, moving the pier the least bit. The moon was a dark red—because of the atmosphere, Charles said. He said it looks big at the horizon because it's magnified by the air, which I'd never thought about. I always thought the orbit was closer when it came up, and then moved away. It sure *looks* that way. Charles said the red was because of chemicals and such in the atmosphere. He knows about stuff I never think about. Anyway, the moon got whiter and higher and soon reflected white off the water.

We stood against the rail, pushing our shoulders together, and Charles sung this little song:

I see the moon and the moon sees me.
And the moon sees the one that I want
   to see.
God bless the moon and God bless me.
And God bless the one that I want to
   see.

I love Charles more than anything. Sometimes he's hard to get along with, and sometimes he has some problems with the family, but he makes up for it in all kinds of little ways, and he's always praising my singing to other people. Daddy said he thought Charles had plenty of common sense beneath all that book learning, and then too at the wedding Daddy said he thought Charles was a good man.

We came back home on Saturday and on the way Mama read to us out of a pamphlet she got in a drug store. It was about having a Christian home and the husband's role and the wife's role. I thought it made good sense, but Charles goes into a sermon right there in the back seat about customs being different in Bible times—which is not the point.

After we got back from the beach, and Charles got his rods separated out, and we drove on home and unpacked, and finished eating supper—some chili I froze before we left—Charles says, "I think I'll call Johnny." I had totally forgot to say anything about the vent or ask Charles if Johnny was a minority, but before I could say anything, Charles was on the phone, talking about the beach trip. I was eating peaches for dessert and it didn't seem like Charles minded me sitting there listening.

"She's got blue hair," he said, "and talks more than anybody I ever met." He was talking about you know who: Aunt Naomi, and eyeing me while he sat there, twisting the curly black phone cord around his finger. Then Johnny must have asked Charles what I looked like. "What does *she* look like?" said Charles, and looked at me and winked. "The most beautiful eyes I've ever seen, some kind of blue-green, and her front two teeth tuck back just enough to make her mouth cute, kind of pouty, and besides all that, she has the purest singing voice ever—can bend a note on a country song as good as any blues singer you ever heard. . . . What? No. No bad habits. Wait a minute. Raney, would you please leave the room?" Then he laughed and said I cussed too much which was a flip-flop because Charles is the one who cusses, and then he said the only fault he could think of was I didn't give him any warning when I started a song and that I rubbed my nose straight up with the flat palm of my hand, but that was cute. Then he said none of my other faults were my fault.

I thought about going to the bedroom and listening through the vent, but that wouldn't have been fair. Maybe it would have been fair if Charles was my child. Mama read my mail; but it was for my own interest. She said she wasn't interested from curiosity, but for the sake of my well-being. So since Charles won't my child and did have a peculiar reaction about privacy which I don't understand, I decided I should tell him about the vent when he finished talking. But he talked so *long*. He told about the fish hook in Norris's nose and then went through Uncle Nate's spelling lesson almost word for word and then some more about Aunt Naomi. He had good things to say about Daddy and Aunt Flossie.

When they finished talking, Charles said Johnny said hello.

I asked Charles what I dreaded: "Charles, is Johnny a minority?"

"He's black, if that's what you mean."

A picture flashed in my mind of Mama and Daddy and Mary Faye and Norris and Uncle Nate and Aunt Naomi and Aunt Flossie and maybe a child of ours in the living room with Charles and his best friend, a nigger.

"Did you say something to him about coming here?" I asked.

"No, not tonight. Why?"

"I just wondered."

"Would that be a problem?"

"I don't guess so."

"You don't guess so?"

"Well, Charles, I know you were in the war together and everything but this ain't exactly the war."

"What does that mean?"

"It means—"

"What does that have to do with our friendship?"

"Nothing, but—"

"Then why are we talking about this?"

"Charles. The army has been segregated since 1948, you said, but Listre still has the black laundromat and the white laundromat and nobody complaining—neither side. Johnny might get embarrassed downtown, that's all I'm worried about."

"You mean the army has been *integrated* since 1948."

"That's what I said."

"You said *segregated*."

"Whatever."

"Raney, don't worry about how Johnny might feel. He's sensitive to racial issues. You don't need to talk to a race horse about the race. He's been there."

"What are you talking about?"

"What I'm saying is that Johnny knows about towns like Listre."

"What does that have to do with a race horse?"

"Never mind. Don't worry about it. He's not coming anytime soon as far as I know. He's busy with law school."

What happened with all this conversation about Johnny Dobbs was: I forgot to mention the vent.

6

CHARLES'S MOTHER CALLED ON THE MONDAY after we got back from the beach and said she was going to Connecticut the first week in September to see her sister, Charles's Aunt Sue, and would like to drop by to see us—on the way up (Monday, Monday night, and Tuesday), and on the way back down to Atlanta (Saturday night and Sunday). She asked if it would be all right, if three months had given us enough time to settle in. I told her it had. She said not to do any extra preparing.

Lord, Lord. Last week was the big week. And it was not smooth, like I'd hoped it would be. Charles had that meeting at our house—wouldn't cancel it—on Monday night, then the Sneeds business was all over the newspaper on the following Saturday which we got in a argument about at Sunday dinner at Mama's with Charles's mother sitting right there in the middle of it, taking up for Sneeds. Sneeds runs Daddy's store. Not to speak of the fact that Charles and Millie went to an Episcopal Church Sunday morning—and dragged me along.

I figured from the start we'd put Millie in the guest room. (She told me on the phone, again, to call her Millie.) Charles suggested *we* stay in the guest room and his mama stay in our room. I said a guest is a guest and that his mother was the guest and that's what the room is: a guest room.

Charles said his mother was not used to sleeping on a narrow bed. So I asked him what did he think I was used to sleeping on, and why didn't he just give his mother the whole house and we'd move on down to the Landmark Motel for the duration.

It was a matter of principle for me and I won out.

Friday, before she came on Monday, I vacuumed the whole place, cleaned the window panes in front, shined up the bathroom, and made the guest room a little nicer by putting in the radio alarm clock, our antique brass lamp, a wall mirror, a little table with some fruit in a bowl, and our biggest wedding picture. Then I realized the fruit bowl might draw gnats, so I took that out.

Friday night Charles tells me about this meeting he's planning to have at our house Monday night—whether his mama is there or not. He's joined this thing called a TEA club; he's been to several meetings and it was his turn to have the meeting at our house. The TEA stands for Thrifty Energy Alternatives. I suddenly realized that with people coming to the meeting, and with Charles's mother being there, I'd have to paint, or Charles would have to paint, the living room.

"Charles, if you'll paint that living room some color I can understand then I'll be happy for you to have your meeting here."

"What's wrong with it as it is?"

"Why do you think I've carried back those six sets of drapes?" See, Charles is just like a man. Has no more sense for color schemes than Bill Grogan's goat. "They didn't *go*. Nothing goes with that scum green tint. And Mama said none of them went. And for sure your mother and somebody at the meeting will notice."

"You're telling me you don't want the meeting over here unless I paint the living room?"

"Most certainly. And your mother can't come unless you do."

"Raney. Do you have some color in mind? My God."

"Some off-white without that green in it. And I've told you about cussing in this house."

"You get the paint and I'll paint it."

So I did. Saturday morning. And Charles painted the living room. Saturday afternoon, before he finished, I got these real nice gold and brown drapes that go. Then after that I got my hair done.

Sunday afternoon Charles goes to the Winn Dixie for groceries and comes back with a bottle of wine. He didn't even ask me—just brought it in as bright as day with the groceries, and I found it while I was unpacking.

"Charles, what's this for?"

"The TEA meeting."

"I'd rather not have wine in this house."

"Raney, some of the people coming to the meeting will be bringing wine. I'd like also to have some available—for my own mother, anyway."

"Charles. Why do you need wine at a meeting?"

"To drink."

I didn't say anything else, partly because it involved Charles and his own mother and partly because it won't champagne, which evidently does something to Charles's brain, and partly, I suppose, because I thought of Madora. She drinks wine at meals, like the French, and she poured me some one afternoon a couple of weeks ago—by mistake: she knows I don't drink. I took a sip, though, to see what all the fuss was about.

Madora's as fine a Christian as you'll find—judging from what all she does for people, and how good she is to her mama and daddy. I drunk only one sip. I told her it was better than champagne. She said champagne was wine, which surprised me because they don't taste the same at all.

We picked up Millie at the airport at about one o'clock Monday afternoon. She was wearing dark green slacks and a blouse she seemed too old for, and she brought me a present—some of those little knitted soap holders I never use.

We waited for her bags forever. She had two great big brown leather suitcases and one little one. Lord knows what all she had in there—for just one week.

To get from the airport to Listre you have to go through Bethel, so on the way home we stopped in at Mama's for a few minutes. Mama had insisted, and I thought it was a good idea.

Mama and Aunt Naomi were there, sitting in the living room, talking. They had been to a sale at Belks.

Everybody said hello to everybody and we all sat down and Mama said something about the sale. She got a navy blue bedspread for forty percent off and Aunt Naomi got a throw rug and two lamp shades for half price. Then they mentioned that on the way back from the sale they'd stopped by the funeral home to see Hattie Rigsbee who had died of a stroke the day before.

"She looked so good," Mama said. "Her skin was clear, good color, no swelling."

"I've seen them awful swelled," says Aunt Naomi. "They say it happens worse when they have a heart attack and nobody gets there right away. I remember Wingate Bryant looked awful. They figured he died right after he went to bed, laid there all night and when Rose got up to go to work she figured he was still asleep, until she brought him a plate of spaghetti at lunch and there he was: still in bed. She worked at the school cafeteria," she said to Millie, "across the street, and would bring him a plate of whatever they had. He was retired. From the telephone company."

"I remember that," says Mama. "You know, I do believe Hattie Rigsbee, today, was about the best looking corpse I've ever seen." She looked straight at Millie, then at Charles, to get them in the conversation.

Charles stands up and walks to the kitchen. I could tell he was mad about something; but Lord knows, I didn't know what, and I hoped Mama and Aunt Naomi and Millie hadn't noticed.

"Let me put on some coffee," I said, "and see if I can rustle up some cookies." I followed Charles on back to the kitchen and whispered, "Charles, what in the world is the matter with you?"

"What's the matter?" he whispers, staring. "What's the matter? Did you hear what she said?"

"Who?" I whispered.

"Who? Who? Your mother."

"About what?"

"About what?" he whispers louder. "About the corpse looking good and all that."

"Well, I guess I did. I was sitting there, won't I? What in the world was wrong with that?"

"What's wrong with it? It's uncivilized—that's what's wrong with it. Raney, the body in the funeral home is not the person. It's the person's body. Why can't your mother talk about the person, for God's sake?"

"Don't you use profanity in this kitchen. And don't get uppity because your mother's here. What do you expect? They were being respectful of Hattie Rigsbee. That's all. I'll bet you didn't even know she died."

"Respect is not the word. Morbid is the word. No, I didn't know Hattie Rigsbee died. I didn't even know Hattie Rigsbee. I didn't even know Hattie Rigsbee was *born*."

"Well, you should have. You been living around here long enough." I was looking for cookies as hard as I could.

"Raney, we don't live around here. We live in Listre."

87

About that time I heard Mama coming down the hall. She came on in the kitchen. "Look, it's no need to mess with coffee," she said. "Mrs. Shepherd says she needs to get on over to y'all's house and get settled. Next Sunday you're all invited over here after church for dinner. Her airplane don't leave until six-thirty so it'll work out just right. And we can all go to church together Sunday morning."

We drove home and got Millie and all her bags settled in the guest room. I'd planned to fix a meatloaf for supper but remembered Sunday about her being a vegetarian. Charles said to fix omelettes but I'd never cooked a omelette so I had to call Madora for a recipe. I practiced Sunday night, so the real thing Monday night turned out pretty good. Millie helped.

Charles had cooked—of all things—one of Aunt Flossie's apple pies. He got her to show him exactly how to cook one—he likes them so much. After his mama had a piece she raved about it and asked *me* what the recipe was. That Charles just sat there smiling and did not say one thing until I explained to Millie that Charles fixed it, not me. She thought I was kidding until Charles talked through about the ingredients and how you fix it. I didn't dare mention that I hadn't ever taken on any kind of pie. This one was good. It was a little tart, but it was good.

I was just beginning to relax when Millie asks,

"Is there an Episcopal church nearby?" I had forgot about her changing over to the Episcopals.

"There's one in White Level," says Charles. "Sara—at the library—goes there."

"You're more than welcome to come to our church," I said. "And since we're going to eat at Mama's, we'll be close by."

"I really like the formality of the Episcopal service," says Millie. "I've gotten used to it. Charles, give them a call this week and if they're celebrating Eucharist Sunday morning around ten or eleven, I could slip over for that."

I didn't know what a Eucharist was. Likely as not they'd be celebrating something.

"Or," she says, "if you two like, you could come along with me."

"I don't think I could go to an Episcopal church," I said.

"Why not?" they both said.

"They're against some of the things we believe in most."

"What do you mean by that?" said Charles.

"Well, they serve real wine at the Lord's supper. And they have priests, don't they?"

"Yes," said Millie.

"Well, I don't especially approve of the way priests drink."

"Jesus drank—if that's what you mean—as I understand it," she says.

"I don't think so."

"Well, he turned the water into wine at the wedding feast."

"Yes, but that was grape juice."

"Grape juice?"

"If Jesus turned water into wine on the spot," I said, "it had to be grape juice because it didn't have time to ferment."

There was a pause.

"If Jesus could make wine," says *Charles* (you could tell whose side he was on), "he could just as easily make it fermented as not, couldn't he? Why mess around with half a miracle?"

"I've been going to Bethel Free Will Baptist Church for twenty-four years now," I said, "and Mr. Brooks, Mr. Tolley, Mr. Honneycutt, and all these other men have been studying the Bible for all their lives and they say it's grape juice. All added together they've probably studied the Bible over a hundred years. I'm not going to sit in my own kitchen and go against that."

"But there are Buddhist monks," says Charles, "who have studied religion for an accumulation of millions of years and they say Jesus was only a holy man and not the son of God. You can find anybody who's studied something for X number of years. I'm not sure what that proves."

"These Buddhist monks were not studying the Bible," I said. "They were studying the *Koran*. We talked about that in Sunday School."

"I don't think they were studying the *Koran*,"

says Mrs. Shepherd. "You're talking about Islam."

"Well, the point is: I'm not talking about the Bible. If it's not in the Bible I'm not interested in it because if I have to stop believing in the Bible I might as well stop living on earth."

"Here, let's get the dishes washed up," says Mrs. Shepherd. "I appreciate your faith—I guess it's a small matter anyway. Sometimes I think we spend too much time on relatively picky religious matters."

It won't no *picky* matter to me.

While we were cleaning up I saw where Charles got his habit of taking the strainer out of the sink and leaving it out, and turning on the faucet and leaving it on. But I didn't say anything. She was nice to help.

Before we finished cleaning up, somebody knocked on the front door. That durn TEA Club meeting. I felt like I hadn't had time to get my bearings.

The meeting was something, and Millie joined in just like she knew everybody.

There was this woman dressed in rags who brought her baby in a sack on her back. Looked like she'd just walked away from a plane crash with her baby all tangled up in her clothes. What's more, she was cock-eyed. Looked like she was looking in two directions at once. Like those pictures of John Kennedy.

There were more unusual people there. But listen to what the meeting was about: they all, including Charles, and his mama, just flown in from Atlanta, are dead set against the Ferris-Jones nuclear power plant being built north of here.

That takes a lot a gall. These scientists have been working for years to get this plant built and Charles and these, well . . . a couple of them looked like hippies to me, and there was a doctor and two college teachers who looked like they don't eat right and the one with the baby—they all get together and in about fifteen minutes decide that the nuclear power plant has got to go. Has got to *go,* mind you.

They haven't hurt anything at the power plant. And electricity certainly has to come from somewhere.

I was in Pope's the other day and the mayor, Mr. Crenshaw, was talking to Mrs. Moss. He said the power plant was the best thing that ever happened to Listre—that it would bring new jobs and make taxes lower.

Now he's the mayor. He's somebody I can listen to. Somebody with a respectable position in the community who *has* to know what he's talking about, else he wouldn't be mayor.

Sometimes I believe these hippies and college professors sit around and frown and complain about what's helping a community most.

Look at the war. These hippies and such were

telling the people who knew the most about it how to run it. So we lost. Now they're doing the same thing with this power plant. Do you see the people from the power plant telling the hippies how to be hippies? No, because they don't know anything about it. So they keep their mouths shut.

Charles told me I could come up front to the meeting but I stayed back in the kitchen. After about thirty minutes, Millie did come back and talk to me about how nice Charles and me had fixed up the house. She had a glass of wine, but that's the only one she drunk as far as I know. I never thought I'd see wine under a roof I lived under. Live and learn. I won't be a prude; but I do have principles and I will certainly keep close guard on what goes on. We're not going to have any alcohol under this roof for more than twelve hours, and otherwise only on some special occasions of Charles's. And when we have a child we'll have to discuss the whole thing very seriously. I never saw a drop of alcohol at home except in a bottle Uncle Nate brought in.

I told Millie about Charles painting the living room and she thought it was funny about not being able to find any drapes to go with the old paint. She said Charles had a good "role model" for fixing up around the house because Bill, Dr. Shepherd, had always helped her. I thought about Daddy. He's never done anything, as far as I can remember, inside the house. He works outside, but not inside. I don't think Mama wants him working in the house. She certainly never lets anybody do anything in the kitchen.

Charles won't do a thing outside but pull up crabgrass out of the sidewalk cracks once in a while. I don't know why he gets such a kick out of that. I think it's connected somehow to his strange ideas about germs. He buys these big jars of alcohol to clean the bathroom sink with. I've seen him through the bathroom door—through the crack. He'll scrub around the hole in the bottom of the sink with a ball of cotton soaked in alcohol. Lord knows where else he scrubs. I'll bet he goes through a bottle of alcohol every two weeks. I go in there some mornings and it smells like County Hospital. I started to ask Millie about that but I didn't. Maybe he got it from her. (It's funny what all you find out about your husband after you get married.)

When they finished the meeting, Charles came back to the kitchen and showed me this letter they wrote with Charles's named signed. Charles asked me what I thought. I said if they all wrote it, why didn't they all sign it? This is the letter. Millie told him a couple of words to change.

DEAR EDITOR:

A state geologist has recently claimed that an area near the proposed Ferris-Jones nuclear power plant is ideal for a hazardous waste disposal site. One of the reasons given is the low population of the area. I suppose the reasoning is that if there are problems, then fewer people will suffer.

It occurs to me that any reason to NOT put something in a highly populated area should also be a good reason NOT to put it in an area of low population.

The sad fact is that problems of nuclear waste disposal are not solved. This generation should not be making decisions that will cause future generations to suffer horrible consequences.

Charles Shepherd

Charles took off work Tuesday afternoon; we took his mama to the airport; and when we got back home we had a little talk which turned into a argument.

I merely asked Charles why he has to be friends with these college professors and such— why he can't be friends with my friends. He went with me *once* to see Madora and her husband, Larry. And Sandra and Billy Ferrell have asked us over for supper twice and he wouldn't go either time. I know they won't ask us again.

"*These* people *think*," he says.

"Think?" I said. "Who *don't* think? Everybody thinks."

"I mean think about something important,

something beyond the confines of their own lives."

"What is that supposed to mean?"

"It means getting beyond Listre and Bethel. That's what it means. Raney, the way it works is this: small people talk about themselves; mediocre people talk about other people; and thinking people talk about ideas."

"What does that have to do with anything?" I said. See, what happens is: Charles spouts out this stuff he's read in the library and expects the words to be formed in gold in my head. But I'm sorry.

"It has to do with who I want to be friends with," says Charles. "Madora and—what's his name?—Larry are not interested in anything outside their kitchen, living room, and bedroom."

"I'll have you know," I said, "that Madora and Larry go to Bethel Free Will Baptist Church. Don't tell me that Jesus Christ is only in their kitchen, living room, and bedroom."

"The problem," says Charles, "the whole problem is just that: Jesus wouldn't have a kitchen, living room, and bedroom."

"He would if he lived in Bethel." I tried to let that sink in. "No matter what your mama thinks."

"Why are you bringing her into this?" (I wasn't sure.) "Raney. Jesus Christ was a radical. If the people at Bethel Free Will Baptist met Jesus they'd laugh at him . . . or lynch him."

"A radical? Charles, I had a personal experience with Jesus Christ when I was twelve years old. He wasn't a radical then. And I did not laugh. As a matter of fact, I cried."

"Were you saved, Raney? Is that it? Were you saved and now you're going to heaven and nothing else matters?"

"Charles," I said, and I was mad, "you can run down whoever and whatever you want to, but when you run down my experience with Jesus Christ you are putting yourself below the belly of a hog." I was tore up. I had to cry. I walked out of the kitchen, into the bedroom and slammed the door with both hands as hard as I could; and Charles goes out the front door and drives off. And didn't come back for thirty minutes.

7

WE DIDN'T SPEAK WEDNESDAY OR THURSDAY, but had started warming up some on Friday. Then Friday night we went to see a movie—some awful thing Charles wanted to see—and then Saturday morning the Sneeds business was all over *The Hansen County Pilot.* As I said, Sneeds runs Daddy's store. Sneeds Perry. I don't know him except from when I go in the store. He's always seemed nice.

What he did was get arrested in Raleigh at two

A.M. Friday night for trying to pick up this woman he *thought* was a you-know-what but instead was a policewoman. They caught him red-handed. And then the whole subject had to come up at Sunday dinner with Mrs.—, with Millie, there visiting.

She came back Saturday night on the airplane, which was late, and I could of sworn I smelled liquor on her breath. Then we had to wait for all those suitcases, which we loaded into the trunk and carted home and into the guest room again.

Charles had found out that the Episcopal service started at 10:30 A.M. Sunday and that they were having that Eucharist, so they decided they'd go for sure and Millie wanted to know if I was going with them. They seemed like they wanted me to, so I said yes. I wanted to see what the service was like, if nothing else.

The service was the most unusual church service you've ever seen. First of all, I didn't know any of the hymns, and *neither did the regular people there.* You'd expect the regular people there to know their own hymns. They wandered all around on notes that didn't have anything to do with the melody and, all in all, didn't sing with any spunk. And they kept kneeling on these teenie-tiny benches. It was up and down, up and down. I got right nervous looking out the corner of my eye to see when it was up and when it was down.

The priest had a yellow robe with a butterfly on the back. Now that is plum sacrilegious if you ask me. A house of worship is no place to play Halloween.

One of the most surprising things of all was that the very thing you come to church to hear wasn't there. A sermon. There was no sermon. The priest talked about three minutes on hope and people in the ghettos, which may have been a sermon to him, but not to me.

They had the Lord's supper, but they didn't pass it around. You had to go up front, kneel down (of course), and get it.

I was a little nervous about drinking real wine in church. But when I thought about it I ended up figuring maybe that was the best place to do it and God would forgive me. It was red wine and about knocked my socks off. It was stronger somehow than Madora's white wine and that expensive stuff that I tried in the kitchen at Charles's TEA party. (That bottle had the price tag on it. Six dollars and something. It seemed like to me it should have cost less because it kind of disappeared once you got it in your mouth.) I want you to know the priest gulped down every bit that was left over at the end. That was an education to me.

All in all, it just wasn't *set up* like a church service. I must admit, several people were nice after the service, but most of them had Yankee accents. They were probably people who've come down to work at the new G.E. plant outside White Level.

Charles said he liked it—that it was "formal." I didn't see anything formal about it. It was confusing to me.

Aunt Naomi and Aunt Flossie were at Mama's for Sunday dinner, along with the rest of us. Everybody seemed happy to see Millie and she seemed likewise. I was a little tense. For one thing I was worried that the Sneeds business would come up, but I figured it wouldn't—not at Sunday dinner.

We got seated, Mama asked Charles to say the blessing; he did; and we started helping ourselves.

I passed the okra to Aunt Naomi. She helped her plate and says, "You want some okra, son?" and passed the bowl to Charles. "We won't get much more this year."

"No, thanks," said Charles.

"No? You don't like okra?"

"Nope."

"Well, I declare. That's surprising. Have you ever had it fried before?"

"I can't remember. I don't think so. I've had it boiled."

"You hadn't ever fried any okra for this boy?" Mama says to Millie.

"We've never been much on okra, somehow," says Millie.

"Well, you ain't had nothing until you've had some good fried okra," says Aunt Naomi, and she drops a piece onto Charles's plate.

"I really don't care for any."

"I remember when I was a little girl no older than Mary Faye there," says Aunt Naomi. "I couldn't stand boiled okra because it was so slimy. For some reason, that's the only way my mama ever fixed it. So I know what you mean. Then when I was, oh, about a teenager, I got aholt of some good fried okra. Mercy me—better than pop corn, with just a tiny hint of fried oyster flavor. Do you like fried oysters?"

"Sure do," said Charles. He was staring at the piece of fried okra on his plate.

"Pop corn?"

"Sure do."

"Well, then, you'll love fried okra. Go ahead, try it."

"I really don't care for any."

"Aw, go ahead. You'll love it; I guarantee. Then when you go home your mama can fix it for you, can't you, Millie?"

"Sure."

Charles ate the piece of okra. It *was* good okra.

"Now, ain't that good?" says Aunt Naomi.

"It was pretty good," says Charles.

Aunt Naomi gets the bowl and hands it to Charles. "Well, here, get you out some."

"No thanks," said Charles. "I'm just fine. I really don't care for any."

"Well, I declare," says Aunt Naomi. "I'm surprised. I thought for sure you'd love it."

Charles put the bowl back and Daddy asked him if he saw the Braves game Saturday and they started talking while Aunt Naomi says, "I don't know what I'd do without my fried okra. That and turnip salet. Why I could make a meal off turnip salet and cornbread, two meals a day for a month. There just ain't *nothing* better. Nothing. Doris, your favorite was always cabbage, won't it?"

"I always liked turnip salet too."

"I hate it," said Mary Faye.

"You hate everything," said Norris.

"I do not."

"Do too."

"Do not."

"Hush," says Mama.

"Y'all went to the Episcopal church in White Level?" says Aunt Naomi. She was looking at Millie.

"Sure did. It was really nice."

Nobody said anything.

"Don't they have a priest like the Catholics?" said Mama.

"Yes, they do," said Millie. "I think their duties might be a bit different, though."

102

"Don't they make them preach in a certain town where they assign them—like in the army?" says Aunt Naomi.

"I don't think they do."

"They don't," says Charles.

"I've made many a meal on turnip salet and cornbread," says Uncle Nate. He had his hair slicked straight back, like always, and was wearing a white starched shirt with the collar open. "And Aunt Annie's nigger, Monkey— remember how he used to all the time talk about drinking turnip green pot liquor?"

That got Charles's and Millie's attention. I was afraid Charles was going to go into his speech about saying "nigger" but he didn't, thank goodness. And Millie didn't, thank goodness. (Charles is sitting there with a big hunk of cream potatoes on his plate, no gravy, two pieces of chicken, a piece of roast beef, a pickle and a piece of cornbread and a roll. No vegetables. He will not get any healthy recipes from Aunt Flossie: only apple pie, fried chicken, and such. It's a wonder he don't get pimples—again. You can tell when he had them a little bit when he was a teenager. Pock marks. I can't imagine how he gets his system cleaned out. It looks like somebody who works in a library would have more sense about what to eat. And Charles ain't the type to shun new things. His mother, of course, had just the opposite: a plate full of vegetables.)

"What's pot liquor?" says Charles to Uncle Nate.

Uncle Nate had his mouth full, which don't usually stop him from talking—as Charles has pointed out to me on the way home so many times now that *I* notice. But this time he kept chewing and didn't answer.

Aunt Flossie answered: "It's what's left in the pot after cooking cabbage—usually cabbage. Course I've seen collard and turnip green pot liquor."

"That sounds interesting," says Charles.

"Did he *look* like a monkey?" asks Norris.

"You know," said Uncle Nate, swallowing his potatoes, "Uncle Springer took Monkey to Raleigh one Christmas to sell quail and they—"

"Did he *look* like a monkey?"

"No, that was just his name, I reckon. Anyway, they got snowed in and there was a light bulb in the room where they spent the night in somebody's house. For some reason Monkey ended up staying with Uncle Springer in the same room. Anyway, Uncle Springer hadn't ever seen a light bulb and of course Monkey hadn't and they didn't know it had a durn switch on it to cut it off and so before they went to bed—I imagine Monkey slept on the floor—before they went to bed they put a chest of drawers up on another table and some chairs and so on and put the durn light bulb—course they didn't know it unscrewed either—they put the durn light bulb in the top drawer and closed it and then went to bed and got a good night's sleep."

I'd heard that story once or twice but I knew Charles and Millie hadn't. It's a funny story but of course Charles don't like to hear nothing about niggers unless it's how Martin Luther King laid down in some restaurant or something. As I said, he has this thing.

"Wadn't that terrible about Sneeds Perry?" says Aunt Naomi.

Nobody said anything. Somebody passed something and a few forks hit plates.

"What happened to Mr. Perry?" asked Norris.

Nobody said anything and Norris looked around at everybody. "What happened to Mr. Perry?" he said again.

It flashed through my mind: Sneeds paying one of those women to do what Charles had said for us to do on our honeymoon. "He got in trouble," I said. "For being where he ought not to be and doing what he ought not to do."

"What did he do?" asked Norris.

"He solicited something from a policewoman which he thought he was soliciting from a woman of the night," said Uncle Nate.

"A witch?" said Norris.

"I wouldn't say that."

"I think if a man wants to ruin his life in one night by breaking the law, then that's the chance he takes," said Mama.

"Do you think he wanted to ruin his life?" said Charles. "That's not exactly what he had in mind, do you think?"

"That's what happened," said Aunt Naomi. "Now he won't be able to get a job within fifty miles—at any place respectable that is. It's a good thing he don't have a family." Aunt Naomi looked at Daddy. "You will have to let him go."

"I ain't decided," said Daddy.

"Daddy, he was arrested," I said.

"You're going to let him keep working out at the store?" said Mama.

"Well, I hadn't thought about—"

"Thurman, you read what he did."

"I know I read what he did. He ain't been tried yet either."

"He won't buying peaches," said Aunt Naomi.

"Peaches?" said Uncle Nate.

"Daddy," I said, "it seems like he'd hurt business with a criminal record."

"It's a misdemeanor, I think," said Charles.

"What's a misdemeanor?" said Norris.

"Hush a minute, Norris," said Mama. "It's a minor crime."

"What did he do?" said Norris.

"He didn't do anything that would have been a great harm to anybody," said Charles.

I thought, "*Charles,* you talk about *harm,* about *not harming*—after that on our honeymoon!"

106

"He broke God's law, that's what he did," said Aunt Naomi.

"I thought for sure you'd fire him, Thurman," said Mama.

"I'm not going to fire a man that ain't been convicted."

We were quiet for a minute.

"Didn't your church group do a thing on victimless crimes?" Charles asked his mama. "It's a pretty interesting perspective."

"Well, yes. The idea was, really, that some acts—without victims—ought to have a low priority on the list of things demanding law enforcement. That is, those crimes would be attended only after the crimes with victims were tended to. That way people would actually be better protected in the long run, because the police would spend more time solving robbery and assault cases and the like, and institutions like churches and mental health clinics could concentrate on the victimless crimes—given the proper support, of course."

It flashed in my mind again about what these prostitutes probably do, and I wondered if Mrs. Shepherd maybe had any idea, and I wondered what she thought about all that. She might think it's okay! I wondered if some of Charles's attitudes could have somehow come from her—if she had the same weakness Charles had. If Charles's weakness came from her! I remembered her and Mr. Shepherd hugging and kissing in front of everybody at the wedding. Putting on like that. I wondered about all the connections. How can you tell? You can't ask!

"I don't know what victims has to do with all this," said Aunt Naomi. "You don't need to have a victim to break the word of God."

"If a you-know-what is not a victim," says Mama, "I don't know who is—but I haven't studied all that about different kinds of crimes."

"Daddy," I said, "what if he is convicted? You'll fire him then, won't you? I mean if he's convicted."

"I don't see what difference it makes whether he's convicted. He done it. Anybody knows that," says Aunt Naomi.

"Well," says Daddy. "I'd want to wait and see what happens."

I had never thought about Daddy keeping somebody on the job who'd do something like that. But the problem is: it didn't seem to make any difference to about half the table sitting in my own mama's house for Sunday dinner, every one kin to me in some way. I don't understand why people won't take a stand where they ought to. Especially my own daddy.

"It's your store," says Mama.

Things got quiet again, except for forks hitting on dishes and Uncle Nate chewing with his mouth open.

"Millie, did you hear about Norris getting the fishing hook hung in his nose at the beach?" said Aunt Flossie.

"Yes, I did. Charles told me on the phone. That must have been something. Were you afraid, Norris?"

"I was afraid when it first happened. I thought a bird or something had flew up my nose."

We all laughed and then Uncle Nate told about the time one of Uncle Springer's boys told his little brother to stick his tongue to a froze ax. We'd all heard it but Millie and Charles hadn't. That got Uncle Nate into telling about the first car Uncle Springer ever saw that had a rear view mirror on the inside and Uncle Springer says, "I comb my hair *before* I leave home."

Uncle Springer was the one who was so bashful that on his wedding night he peed down his leg into the pot so he wouldn't make any noise. So they *say*.

The stories eased the tension some. For me, anyway. We finished eating; Mama and Aunt Flossie cleaned up; then we sat and talked for awhile. At about two-thirty we left and drove home. I could tell Charles was getting tired of sitting and talking. Then at about five o'clock we took Millie and those big suitcases to the airport.

Just before she got on the plane, she gave me a big hug and a kiss. I hugged her back but didn't

109

have time to figure out where to kiss her before we'd turned each other loose. I've just never hugged and kissed people I don't know real well. Or people I do know real well, for that matter.

8

IT WON'T SNEEDS THEY ARRESTED. IT WAS Sam Perry, Sneeds's first cousin. The newspaper got it mixed up because Sam signed Sneeds's name and gave Sneeds's address, and at the police station he actually had the driver's license that Sneeds thought he'd lost. Daddy said Sam told Sneeds he didn't want his wife and kids to find out and he figured Sneeds wouldn't mind. Sneeds told Daddy that Sam had done the same thing before and so he wadn't too surprised. I can't believe somebody would do something like that to their own cousin.

I was in the store Saturday morning trying to figure out whether I should mention the whole thing to Sneeds when Charles called and said to call Mama. I did, and she wanted to know if I could come over and stay with Norris and Mary Faye that afternoon while she went to sit with Uncle Newton—while Aunt Minnie helped with the church barbecue. Aunt Minnie is Daddy's sister and has had an awful time taking care of Uncle Newton. She has to stay with him all the time. Charles was supposed to play tennis that afternoon with somebody from the library, so I said I'd be glad to come over and help out.

The only reason Mama wanted me to stay is because Uncle Nate had disappeared for two days and she was afraid he might come riding up in a Yellow Cab, drunk, with nobody at home but Mary Faye and Norris.

So I went over Saturday at about two. Right before Mama drove off she blew the police whistle for Mary Faye and Norris, who were up the road at Teresa Campbell's house, to come on home. When she saw them coming—on their bicycles—she got in the car and drove off.

She was just out of sight around the curve when Norris, going about fifty miles an hour, turned, or tried to turn, into the driveway—on his Piggly Wiggly Special (that bike he won at the Piggly Wiggly opening: with a row of little red glass rubies up and down the fenders, and a saddle bag, and black rubber mud flaps, and sticking right out front under where the handlebars come together, this solid cast, little brown and white pig head). He had just passed Mary Faye, going as fast as he could, standing up. Then he sat back down and turned about one foot short of the edge of the driveway. The front wheel dipped into the ditch; the bike stopped; and he made a arc through the air—landing full on his thumb.

When I got to him he was sitting on the ground

looking at his right hand like he'd never seen it before. His thumb was drooped down like a broke tree limb, and where it connected to his hand looked like a golf ball.

Mary Faye was standing there. "That thumb is broke, Norris. You can't move it, can you?"

Norris looked up at her, then at me, then at his thumb, and started bawling. I gathered myself as best I could. "Come on," I said. "We'll take you to emergency, right now. Do you hurt anywhere else?" All I could do was take him to the emergency room. That was the only thing to do. His hand looked awful.

Norris said No he wadn't hurting anywhere else, and stood up slow, crying, holding his hurt hand up and in front with his other hand like he was carrying a bunch of flowers.

We hadn't walked no more than ten steps when a Yellow Cab pulls into the driveway. It was like the ocean had pulled in and was about to drown everything. I just stopped and stood there. "Oh *no,*" says Mary Faye.

"Y'all stay right here," I said. It was clear I had to take over. I'd have to do what Mama would do, which was take over. I walked to the driver's side of the taxi. The driver was a pale little man with short red and gray hair, a scrawny mustache, and no teeth. "Howdy," I said.

"Howdy, ma'am."

I looked through at Uncle Nate sitting on the

passenger side. His head was down like he was asleep. "Uncle Nate, you ought to be ashamed of yourself." He didn't even look up. "Mary Faye, y'all go on up and sit down on the porch. No, wait a minute. Go in and call Aunt Minnie and tell her to tell Mama, when she gets there, to come back home and sit with Uncle Nate—that it looks like Norris broke his thumb and I got to take him to emergency. Tell her his thumb is all that's hurt. Tell her it might just be out of place. Ask Aunt Minnie if she minds being a little late for the barbecue."

"I don't know the number."

"It's in that address thing—under Minnie."

"Sir," I said to the cab driver. "Can you wait one minute while I figure out what to do?"

"No problem. Meter's running."

"Uncle Nate, I ought to call the sheriff right now. If I didn't have to take care of Norris, I would."

Uncle Nate looked up. "Where's Doris at?"

"She's on the way to Aunt Minnie's, to sit with Uncle Newton."

"How's ole Newt?"

"He's okay, I guess. He's *sober.* That's for sure."

"Me and Newt were in the war together," Uncle Nate said to the cab driver.

"Uncle Nate, he don't care. Can you get out? You ought to be ashamed of yourself. I'm in the middle of Norris's broke thumb and here you show up, drunk, and probably without one cent. Have you got any money?"

Uncle Nate stuck his hand down in his front pocket.

"He said his sister would pay," said the cab driver.

"That's what I figured," I said.

Mary Faye came out. "The line's busy."

Norris was sitting on the front steps. He started crying, and then hollering. "Oh, it's starting to hurt! Ohhhh!" He was holding his hand down between his legs, rocking back and forth, looking at me.

"Elevate it—hold it up," I said.

"They might have to take it off," said Mary Faye.

I was standing there in the front yard, knowing I had to make a decision. I decided Uncle Nate would have to go to the emergency room with us. There was nothing else to do. I went around to the passenger side and opened the door. Or I could call the sheriff. Or I could send him over to Uncle Newton's in the taxi and let Mama look after him. No, that would get Uncle Newton all upset. But Uncle Nate was about asleep. That was good. I figured if he'd stay in the car at emergency, everything would be okay.

"Sir, would you please help me get him in the back seat of my car over there."

"Yeah, I'll help," said the cab driver. "That's a broke thumb if ever I seen one." He'd caught a glimpse of Norris's thumb.

"I know. I've got to get him to emergency."

We got Uncle Nate out of the taxi and into the back seat of my car. He went right on down, laying on his side in the seat with his feet in the floor. His shirt tail was out on the side and his hair was pushed up in back with little flecks of white thread or something all in there.

I paid the taxi driver; Norris and Mary Faye got in the car, up front with me.

Norris stopped crying about halfway to the emergency room, and when we turned into the hospital driveway, Uncle Nate sat up. "Is Newt up here?" he said.

"Uncle Newton's at home, Uncle Nate. Norris hurt his thumb and we're having to take him to emergency."

"Less see that thumb, boy."

Norris held up his thumb.

"Oh, that ain't nothing." He leaned up right behind me. "Raney." I could smell his breath. I was almost afraid of him. I had this flash thought of him grabbing me around the neck, although Uncle Nate is normally pretty gentle, drunk or sober, except when he's drunk and gets mad and curses. "Raney, where's Doris?"

"She's at Uncle Newton's. I told you a minute ago."

We pulled the car up close to the emergency room door and stopped. "Now, Uncle Nate, you stay right here. I'll be right back."

"Does Mary Faye and Norris remember me and Newt were in the war together?"

"Yessir," I said. "Now please stay in the back seat, Uncle Nate. Will you do that? I'll be right back."

"I certainly will. You know I love you, Raney."

I got out and came around and opened the door for Norris. He had stopped crying. He got out, holding his hand up with that thumb dangling, and we all started in, except for Uncle Nate. I looked back. He was sitting with his head slumped over.

When we got to the emergency room door, I said, "Mary Faye, stand right here at the door, and if Uncle Nate gets out of the car, you come in and tell me."

"I want to go in."

"Mary Faye."

"I won't know where you're at," she said.

"Raney, what are they going to do to it?" says Norris, looking up at me with bloodshot eyes.

"Wait a minute, Norris." I looked at Mary Faye. "Do what you have to do, Mary Faye—for goodness sakes. They're going to fix it, Norris."

We all three went in through the door. Some people were sitting in chairs and there was a big nurse across the room at a desk. Two nigger

116

orderlies were sitting behind her—smoking cigarettes and wearing those little green scarf hats with strings hanging down beside their ears.

We walked up to the desk. The nurse asked a bunch of questions and about the time I finished answering them all I hear this loud, banging crash behind me at the door. I look, and there's Uncle Nate: sitting on the floor, half in and half out the emergency room door. Some woman wearing a dress, brown shoes, and white socks jumped up and rushed over to him. I started toward him, but Norris hollered, "Raney, wait a minute, what are they going to do? It hurts!" The orderlies stood up to look at Uncle Nate.

The woman with white socks said, "This man needs help! His eyeballs is rolled back!" The orderlies started running toward Uncle Nate, pushing a table-bed. I heard the woman say, "I think he had a stroke," and before I could say anything—Norris was holding on to my arm with his good hand—the orderlies had Uncle Nate on the bed, rolling him right by me. "Wait a minute, he's my uncle!" I said. They stopped. And here Uncle Nate sort of came around and started cussing the orderlies terrible.

"Uncle Nate stop that right now or I'm going to call Dorcus Kerr to come get you and take you to jail. You all unstrap him from there."

"That woman said he had a stroke," said one orderly.

"Don't let him off there," said the other one.

"I thought you were with this boy," said the nurse to me.

"Raney, I don't want to get it operated on," said Norris.

"You *better* be *quiet,*" said Mary Faye.

"I'm with both of them," I said to the nurse. "This one's drunk; he didn't have a stroke."

One of the orderlies pulled a strap tighter on Uncle Nate. Uncle Nate was cussing him awful. "And where you got Newt?" he said to the one closest to his head.

"I ain't got no Newt. What you talking about, man?"

"Young woman, we're not equipped to handle alcoholism," said the nurse.

"I didn't bring him to the emergency room," I said.

"Who brought this man?" said the nurse to everybody in the emergency room. Then she said to me, "Is your mother here?"

"I'm twenty-four years old," I said.

Norris pulled at my arm. The woman with the white socks came walking up. "I thought he might a had a stroke," she said. "His eyes was rolled back and all. It was that way with my granddaddy. He had a stroke last year and when—"

"I brought him," I said, "but I left him in the car and—"

"Raney!" said Norris.

"Somebody has to take care of his thumb," I said to the nurse.

"I got papers in on him," said the nurse. "The doctor will be here in a minute."

"How do you feel?" said the woman with socks—to Uncle Nate.

"I feel like if I don't get off this goddamned table in five seconds, I'm gone whip ass when I do."

"I'm gonna strap your ass down so tight your eyeballs'll pop out," said the orderly. "Then I'm calling the police."

"*I'll* call the law," I said. "You don't know who to call."

"The hell I don't."

"Wait a minute, Jerry," said the nurse. "I'll call Security."

"Call the goddamned Security," said Uncle Nate.

There was Mary Faye and Norris standing there hearing all that.

"Uncle Nate, please be quiet. You're in trouble. Don't make it worse."

"I was in trouble when I was born."

"Not like you gonna be," said the orderly.

"Stop egging him on," I said.

Up walked the doctor, thank the Lord. The nurse was on the phone: "Donald, send somebody to emergency. We've got a man disturbing the peace."

"What's his name?" said the doctor. He was picking up a clipboard.

"Ask her," said the nurse.

The doctor looked at me.

"Uncle Nate," I said. "Nate Purvis."

"He's your uncle?"

"Yes sir."

"Let me see that thumb, Nate."

"He's Norris."

"I'm Norris," Norris said, his eyes great big.

"Excuse me, Norris. Let me see that thumb." He held Norris by the wrist and turned his hand around. "Hummm. Let's go get an x-ray. *This* man is your uncle, then," he said to me.

"Yes sir, and he's drunk. He shouldn't even be in here. I left him outside."

"Have you got a car?"

"Yes sir."

"I'm Joe Cisco," he said. He smiled and reached out his hand. "Looks like you could use a little help."

I took his hand, tried my best to hold back, but I couldn't help crying. I straightened right back up though.

"I'll be right back and we can get him in your car," he said. Then he took Norris down the hall; Norris looked back over his shoulder—still holding that hand up like he was carrying flowers; the nurse asked the orderlies to sit down; and then Dr. Cisco came back while they were taking the x-ray. He helped me roll Uncle Nate to the car, then get him off the table and in the back seat—with no trouble, since Uncle Nate had passed out. I saw the empty pint in Uncle Nate's back pocket. I hadn't thought to look before. When a security guard walked up, Dr. Cisco explained that everything was all right. Dr. Cisco was a blessing from heaven.

He told us to wait in the car and that after he took care of Norris he'd bring him out. Sometimes I get to thinking there's not one nice person left in the world and then somebody like Dr. Cisco comes along.

It turned out that Norris's thumb was just out of place. It must have been very out of place. Dr. Cisco taped it up over a piece of metal and told me to bring him back in a week unless a problem came up. He stood there at the car and talked a minute.

Uncle Nate won't so simple. He begged me to take him to the liquor store, saying he just needed one more little drink to hold him over. I did not take him, of course.

When we got home he was asleep or passed out. I left him in the car while I called Mama. She called Juanita Bowles to come sit with Uncle Newton and then came on home. We had a terrible time getting Uncle Nate up the front steps.

Daddy came home right after we got Uncle

Nate in the door. "Nate, you're going to get drunk one time too many and get robbed *and* shot instead of just robbed," said Daddy. Uncle Nate's billfold is always empty when he comes home drunk. Uncle Nate started cussing Daddy, which is the first time that's ever happened, as far as I know.

Mama called Dorcus Kerr who came out and arrested Uncle Nate. There was nothing else to do. Uncle Nate spent three days in jail, drying out. That's how long it takes. Mama took him every one of his meals except his last one which was Tuesday lunch. I had to be uptown anyway so I told Mama I could do it and then bring him home when they let him out at three in the afternoon. I'm old enough now.

Dorcus Kerr was at the jail. "I declare, I hate to see this happen, Raney," he said. "When he's sober he's one of the nicest men I know, but I declare, then he has to go and do the way he does; and you all have always been so good to him—your daddy giving him work and all."

I didn't see anybody else in any of the jail cells except Uncle Nate. He was sitting in a chair, leaning back against the wall. His hair was combed straight back with Vitalis, like always, and he was wearing a freshly starched white shirt Mama had brought him. Mr. Kerr opened the door with a big set of keys.

"Hey, girl," said Uncle Nate. "Where's Doris?"

122

"She's at home."

He looked okay except for his eyes which were red and cloudy.

"How do you feel?" I asked.

"I feel pretty good. Raney, I'm sorry. You know I wouldn't do anything in the world to hurt you all."

"I know you wouldn't, Uncle Nate." I started to say, "But you *do—over and over and over.*" Then I saw his hand shaking while he pulled at his ear.

"I've made a decision this time. I'm quitting. I'm getting the shakes. Look at my hands. I can't get them any stiller than that. I'm just going to have to tell myself to quit and then do it."

"You know you can't take that first drink, Uncle Nate. It's all over when you do that. You've got to have the strength to say no. There's plenty of people who do it. And Mama has done everything she can, as you well know."

"She has. She has. She sure has."

"I'm glad you're going to stop, Uncle Nate. You've said that before, though."

"This is the first time I've had the shakes like this. Look at that." He looked at his hands, then at me. "How is Newton? Didn't somebody take him to the hospital Sunday—or Saturday?"

"Nobody took him to the hospital, but he's not doing too good. That was Norris I took. He knocked his thumb out of joint, but it's doing okay."

"He's a little fighter, ain't he?"

"He sure is. Here, you better eat your dinner. I'll be back at three. I need to do a little shopping. You need anything?"

"Some Scholl's footpads. Size 9-C."

I came back at three and picked up Uncle Nate and took him by home and then on out to the store. He usually works out there in the afternoons. He's never been able to do any more than just help out, of course, but it helps Daddy be able to come and go and oversee instead of being there with Sneeds all the time—one of them tending pumps while the other works inside. When Daddy had a chance to get all self-service pumps he turned them down, so he needs Uncle Nate.

PART TWO
A Civil War

1

I FINALLY GOT CHARLES TO JOIN IN ON something that will get his head out of a book. Aunt Flossie organizes a Golden Agers' day every fall and for the past two falls I've helped her. I asked Charles if he'd help us this fall and he said he would.

Mrs. Moss, Mrs. Williams, and Mrs. Clements from our neighborhood are in the Golden Agers and I take them to their meeting the first Thursday morning of each month. They live close to our house and when they come over to visit, Charles'll get up, go to the bedroom, sit and read. He'd rather read a book, written by somebody he don't know, than to sit down and talk to a live human being who's his neighbor.

So I brought it up a few days ago. "Charles," I said, "you'd rather sit down back there in the bedroom and read a book than talk to a live human being like Mrs. Moss."

"I'm not so sure I agree with your assessment of Mrs. Moss," he says.

"What do you mean by that?"

"It means I have had one conversation with Mrs. Moss and one conversation with Mrs. Moss is enough. I am not interested in her falling off the commode and having a hairline rib fracture. I am not interested in her cataract operation. Mrs. Moss is unable to comprehend anything beyond her own problems and you know it."

This is one of the areas of life Charles does not understand. Mama and Aunt Flossie have taught me, for as long as I can remember, to be good to old people. Charles thinks old people are all supposed to grace him with a long conversation on psychology.

Mrs. Moss does talk about herself right much. She'll come over in her apron to borrow a cup of something. One Sunday she borrowed a cup of flour after I saw a bag of Red Band in her shopping cart—on top—at the Piggly Wiggly on Saturday. But the way I figure it is this: Mrs. Moss has had a lifetime of things happening to her and all along she's had these other people— her husband and children—to watch these things happen. So she didn't ever have to *tell* anybody. Then her husband died and her children left and there was nobody around to watch these things happen anymore, so she don't have any way to share *except* to tell. So the thing to do is listen. It's easy to cut her off when she goes on and on. You just start talking about something else. She follows right along.

"She's given me several pints of preserves and one quart of chow-chow," I said. "She can comprehend that."

"Raney, that has nothing to do with the fact that

she is senile and self-centered. There are old people who aren't self-centered, you know."

"Charles, she also showed me how to keep applesauce from turning brown in the jar, and she's going to give me some cactus seeds and she said she'd help me dig up a circle and plant them. And give me some big rocks to go around that. If she's so self-centered, why is she giving me preserves and chow-chow and seeds?"

"Because it's a habit. A life-long habit. If you were Atilla the Hun she'd give you preserves and chow-chow and seeds."

"Charles. Sometimes I wonder about your heart."

"Raney, my heart is all right. What can I do to prove my heart is warm and kind?"

My mind darted around. "Help Aunt Flossie and me with her Golden Agers' day in a couple of weeks. It'll take about an hour next Saturday to ride out to Mr. Earls's to see if he'll shoot his cannon for us. Then the next Saturday help me take some of the Golden Agers out to Mr. Earls's—if he agrees—to watch him shoot his cannon, and then Saturday afternoon we're going to take them to the bluegrass festival, where me and you are going to play anyway. It'll take from about ten to three. All you have to do is just go along."

"Will you worry about my heart if I do?"

"Never again. And you're reading that book on

the Civil War, so you can probably learn something from Mr. Earls."

"Will I have to do something like this every Saturday?"

"No."

Aunt Flossie said she had heard that Mr. Earls didn't have a phone so I might have to ride out to his house to ask him about helping us out. She said he was a Primitive Baptist and shouldn't be any harm, if I wanted to ride out by myself. But Charles rode with me to meet him—this past Saturday morning, one of those hot fall days.

We turned into the driveway of a nice looking brick house, ranch style, with trees, except the leaves hadn't been raked. There was a big flagpole at the mailbox flying the Confederate flag. Charles sees that and goes, "Oh, no," like a paint bucket had fell over.

We stopped in the driveway and got out. A dog came out to meet us. He was a old dog, and didn't even bark. In the carport was a man sitting beside a cannon, working on it. Then I saw a cannon on the front porch and another one out in the back yard. The man got up and walked out to the car. Right off he reminded me of Abraham Lincoln, without a beard. He was over six feet tall, and wearing blue and white striped overalls with a belt holding all these tools. His waist looked like it won't no bigger than mine. His ears stuck straight out and his hair was black and short. I thought: that's the skinniest man I've ever seen in my life. When he got up close I saw that his temples and cheeks were sunk in so that he looked like a skeleton almost. And he didn't have much coloring in his face.

"Howdy," he said. "What can I do for you?" He had a deep business voice. Charles reached out and shook his hand and introduced us.

"We wanted to call, but couldn't find a listing," said Charles.

"I don't have a phone. Don't have a television. I wouldn't have lights if they hadn't already been hooked up when we bought the place. Ain't no need for none of it except for a electric drill and a table saw. I'll use a electric drill and a table saw. But that's it. What can I do for you all?"

I explained about the Golden Agers' Day.

"I'd be happy to help you out. People don't do nothing for old people nowadays. I told Birdie, I said 'Birdie, when the man gets here in the ambulance to take me to one of them nursing homes, if you're living and able, put me in the bed, put a sheet over my head, and tell him I'm dead. And if you ain't able to take care of me then stop feeding me, and if the youngin's won't take care of me, then let me die doing the best I can.'" He looked straight at Charles. "Nothing more than the best we can do is required of any of us. My mama is right there in my living room right now. Far as I know she ain't ever heard a one of these cannons go off, and I shoot one about every day. She does the best she can, which ain't nothing but breathe. Birdie and me do the rest. And the good Lord provides. What time you all want to come out next Saturday?"

"How about ten o'clock?" I said.

"That'll be fine. I'll build a lean-to, start a campfire, and have a regular little show. If there are any men along we'll let them join in. Come here and let me show you where I blew a hole in my tool shop."

I thought: maybe we better think twice.

Mr. Earls had one of those little sheds out back and one side had a big hole in it which he'd covered with clear plastic. "I don't know how in the world it happened," he said. "I had a box of powder and I guess a spark got to it some way. We'd been firing at a reenactment and maybe a spark got in there somewhere and smoltered. I been in the Civil War business over forty year and nothing's blowed up but twice."

"What was the other time?" I asked.

"A cannon. I'd walked about twenty feet from it—to get a drill—and it blew up. Blew a limb out of the tree it was under. Listen, won't you all come in and look at some of my relics?"

We said we'd like to. We walked through the carport door into the kitchen. Mrs. Earls was cooking dinner. Mr. Earls introduced us then took off his belt of tools and dropped it on the bar

132

and said, "Put those tools in the box, honey. Y'all come on in the living room and have a seat."

In the living room, propped up in a brass bed that must not have been polished in ten years was Mr. Earls's mother. Mr. Earls introduced us but she kept looking straight ahead. She had a tiny brown face that looked like a apple that had been on the window sill for about a year.

"There's my children's pictures on the wall," said Mr. Earls. "Didn't a one go to college, thank the good Lord. They all make a good living and are respectful of the things deserving respect."

I wondered if Mrs. Earls was going to put up his tools—why he didn't put up his own tools. Then I heard the tools knocking in a box. She was putting them up.

"What you all want to drink—water, milk, or orange juice?"

We both said orange juice.

"Birdie, bring these folks some orange juice. You folks sit down right over there."

Birdie came in with two glasses of orange juice. "He makes me unload his tools," she said, "then load them back up. I told him just to hang up his belt with the tools in it, but he won't do it." She was a tiny woman who looked like one of those migrant worker women in Charles's photography book.

"Stretches the leather," said Mr. Earls.

"He could lay it down somewhere, couldn't

133

he?" I said to Mrs. Earls. I wanted to even things up a little.

"I don't leave things laying around," said Mr. Earls. "Against my principles. Let me tell you: I model my life after Stonewall Jackson, one of the greatest generals in the history of war. Birdie knows I do, and abides it. And I'll tell you this: the German panzer divisions had Stonewall Jackson to thank. He'll go down with Napoleon. He was a great general, a great man, a Christian."

Birdie brought some cookies. Chocolate chip. Bought.

"Do you all know anything about the Civil War?" says Mr. Earls. "If you don't, you should."

"I've heard about it off and on all my life," I said, "but I don't know much."

"I'm reading a book right now," said Charles.

"Which one?" said Mr. Earls.

"Bruce Carton's."

"Which one?"

"The big one."

"Read Shelby Foote's three when you finish that one. They're the best for an overview." He went on to talk about all these books on the Civil War, about Stonewall Jackson getting shot by his own men, and I don't know what all—something about a secret message wrapped around cigars. Then he brought out all these bullets and pistols and rifles, and finally Mrs. Earls asked us if we wanted to eat dinner. We politely refused and drove on home.

I thought about what a one-two—one on the top, two on the bottom—marriage Mr. and Mrs. Earls had. He was one and she was two. And she seemed perfectly happy. Charles wouldn't ever ask me to hang up a tool belt of his. If he did, he'd be more upset about it than me. At home, inside the house, Mama was one and Daddy was two. It seems like Mrs. Earls and Daddy were born number twos, but Charles . . . I don't know. He was born one and a half, and that don't leave me but one and a half, whether I like it or not. We've talked about it some. It's fair. No doubt about that, but I don't know if it's natural.

We were riding along and Charles says, "Well . . . a real live Rebel."

"What do you mean?"

"That's the mind that ruled the South before the Civil War, I imagine. You heard what he said about blacks being better off before the war than after the war."

"He didn't say 'blacks.'"

"That's what he meant."

"Some of that might be true."

"What do you mean? Are you telling me that slaves were better off than free blacks? Come off it." Charles looked at me. He was holding onto the steering wheel with one hand and his other arm was propped in the window.

"Look at Mrs. Earls," I said. "She's a slave if ever I saw one, and she's a lot happier than your normal 'free hippie.'"

"Raney. This theory about the southern black being better off as a slave is a rationalization. If you found one slave saying he'd rather be a slave than free, then you could account for that through some exceptional circumstance—or ignorance."

"Well, I don't know. I know you don't know everything about Mr. Earls's 'mind.' You don't know nothing about how he took care of his children, about whether he goes to church or not. Aunt Flossie said he was a Primitive Baptist, and they—"

"For the sake of argument, let's suppose he does go to church—every Sunday, Sunday night, and Wednesday night, and for all the sunrise services and whatever the hell else. I'd like to know what that proves, exactly."

"It proves he's in church like the Bible says he's supposed to be. It proves—"

"Wait a minute. Let's take that one. What does that prove?"

"What does what prove?"

"That he's in church like he's supposed to be."

"It proves he's obeying God's word."

"A monkey can obey God's word."

"Don't be ridiculous, Charles."

"I'm merely responding logically to your argument."

"Charles, a monkey can *break* God's word too. And I'd rather have the monkey who kept God's word. This argument don't make sense because a monkey don't even know what God's word is, and a man does, so you can't have a monkey breaking God's word, but you can have a man breaking God's word."

"What about a man who doesn't know God's word—has never heard it. Those kind of men live and die every day."

"We're talking about Mr. Earls who *does* know God's word. Stick to the subject."

"Raney, the whole point—"

"Charles, the whole point is that you think you know what you're talking about and you've just met Mr. Earls and you're jumping to all kinds of conclusions about him."

"Raney, I'm talking about the Civil War. Who do *you* think should have won the war?"

I waited a minute. "I don't know."

"You don't know?"

"I'm not taking a stand either way, Charles. You should have been born a Yankee—that's all I know. Some of my relatives were killed in the Civil War. Who do you think I am, a traitor?"

Charles gave up. We were at home anyway.

Aunt Flossie was real happy to find out that Mr. Earls would help out. After Charles and me had a banana sandwich I drove straight over to tell her. I've finally got Charles to eat peanut butter and potato chips on a banana sandwich—along with mayonnaise. He used to wouldn't eat anything but mayonnaise on one.

2

ON GOLDEN AGERS' DAY, MR. EARLS MET US (we were in three cars and a van) in his Confederate uniform. Birdie was standing beside him in a granny dress and a blue bonnet. On the front porch was Mr. Earls's mama, sitting wrapped up in a quilt and with a tight navy blue knit hat pulled down to her neck. We turned into his driveway and all piled out—thirteen Golden Agers and six people who were helping out.

Down across the yard, close to the woods, was the cannon, and on beyond that in the edge of the woods was a shelter built out of pine tree limbs with a burning campfire close by. Beside the campfire were three bunches of rifles, stacked with their barrels coming together at the tips.

The Channel 9 TV van turned in the driveway. Aunt Flossie had called them and they said they might be able to come.

Mr. Earls was walking around shaking hands with everybody. "Glad you made it. Glad you made it." Birdie headed toward the campfire—to keep it going, I guess.

"Birdie," hollered Mr. Earls, "get those hats and coats out of the lean-to."

Birdie brought Civil War hats and coats and Mr. Earls put them on several of the men, including Charles. Aunt Flossie told the TV men—Bob Ross and a cameraman—that me and Charles had our banjo and guitar in the car and might be willing to do a little back-up music. They asked us if we would and we said we'd be glad to. I got nervous and Charles got fidgety—kept tuning his B string.

Bob Ross got a bunch of people to stand and sit around the campfire, and he put me and Charles off to the side picking "Salt Creek," while he interviewed Mr. Earls and Aunt Flossie about the Civil War and the Golden Agers' day. We played through "Salt Creek" three times before they were through. I asked Bob Ross when it would be on TV and he said Monday night probably. He looked lots older than he does on TV. He seemed like a normal person, though.

The cameraman took a few more shots of people sitting around the campfire and then a close-up of Charles and me picking and singing. Then Mr. Earls says, "Okay, let's fire the cannon. *Birdie, gunpowder.*"

Birdie hurried over to a wooden box, got out a little package, and hurried back to the cannon where Mr. Earls was. He went straight to work while he hollered out for the men in uniform to get a rifle and line up beside the cannon and to be careful because the rifles were loaded. The men ambled over with the rifles. Everybody else stood in a group over toward the cars—to watch. Mr. Earls made a short speech to the group about the use and movement of field artillery in battle. He was wearing a sword which he pulled out and pointed as he talked. The cameraman filmed part of that. Then Mr. Earls starts toward the cannon and says to the cameraman, "Take your picture from anywhere you want to."

"I think I'll stay here," he said. He was over with us watching.

"I ain't shooting nothing but wadding. You could get right out front. The rifles ain't got nothing but wadding, either."

"I think I'll stay here."

Mr. Earls went to work ramming a long stick, with a cloth balled up on the end, down the barrel of the cannon. Then he walked around to the back of the cannon, picked up a smaller stick with cloth on the end—soaked in kerosene, I guess— walked to the campfire, lit the cloth, came back and stood behind the cannon. A fuse was sticking up from the rear of the cannon, looking like a little white rope. The men were lined up on each side of the cannon. "You men back up over here," he said. "No, you. Right. Camera ready? Ladies and gentlemen! Here we go."

Charles was holding a rifle, wearing that little

Rebel hat, standing beside Mr. Goodman, looking at me with his eyes real wide, pretending he was scared to death.

"*Men. Prepare to fire.* Sir. Raise that gun a little if you will. No, not you. Yes, you. Good. *Ready on the left, ready on the right, ready on the firing line. Ready. . . . Aim. . . .*"

Mr. Earls touched the fire to the fuse—which I guess was stuck down into the gunpowder somehow—then stood back. The fuse sparkled and fizzed, and just as the spark reached the cannon he said, *"Fire."*

The rifles fired. The cannon just sat there.

"*Birdie.* Get the drill."

Birdie ran over to the corner of the house, bent over and picked up something, then went running to the cannon with this electric drill with a long orange extension cord dragging along behind.

I got in the front door of the TV van and moved to the back where an extra camera was and sat down on a little bench. About a minute later Charles was in there. "Did you see what he's doing?" said Charles.

"Yes, I did. What's he doing with a drill?"

"I do not know."

I buried my head under my hands and Charles got the giggles. Then I got the giggles. "Charles, I don't want to die in the Civil War." We could hear the high whine of the electric drill.

"Maybe it'll be on TV if we do," said Charles. "I guess I'd better sneak back out there."

"I'm staying put," I said.

In a few minutes I heard another "Ready, aim, fire," and there was a awful loud boom along with the rifles firing. I got out of the van. Everybody was clapping and white smoke was drifting up into the air.

Next was the bluegrass festival. We got everybody loaded into the cars and van and drove to Hardee's for lunch, then out to the Templeton Highlands—two big pastures—for the Fallfest Bluegrass and Gospel Show. Charles and me were scheduled for two o'clock. Mr. Rittle, from church, called us in August and asked us if we wanted a spot on the show; two acts had cancelled. His son, Ferrell, was in charge and had asked him if he knew anybody who could take the places of the cancelled acts. They have it every year in late October, usually the last bluegrass festival around. So since August, I've been promising Mary Faye and Norris that if they'd learn one of our songs they could come up on stage and sing with us. They both have good voices and Mary Faye can sing harmony better than Charles. Charles has to *learn* his part whereas Mary Faye picks it up natural. Well . . . like I do.

The stage was at the bottom of a hill and people

were sitting around on blankets and in lawn chairs. Mary Faye and Norris were there with Mama and Daddy; they had lawn chairs down front. Mr. Rittle saw to it that all the Golden Agers got in free, and the church provided fold-up chairs that we set up a ways behind Mama and Daddy. We got everybody settled at about 1:30. At 2:00 Charles and me went up to play.

Charles is getting better and better on banjo. He's been working on "Devil's Dream" and "Doug's Tune" all summer and they're the two instrumentals we did Saturday. Then I sang "Careless Love," "I'll Go Stepping Too," "Farther Along," "Keep on the Sunny Side," "You Are My Flower," "Fifty Miles of Elbow Room," and "When the Roses Bloom in Dixieland." Just before Mary Faye and Norris came up we did this beautiful song by Alice Gerrard and Hazel Dickens that we've been working on: "West Virgina," with Charles singing harmony. (Charles bought me the album it's on as a surprise. He buys me about one album a month. He'll remember a song I like on the radio and the next thing I know, when I go to bed there's the album under my pillow.)

Then Mary Faye and Norris came up and sang "I'll Fly Away" with us. I was going to dedicate it to the Golden Agers but Charles said I'd better not. I saw why he thought I ought not to, but I decided he was being too sensitive, so I dedicated it to them anyway. They appreciated it.

Norris and Mary Faye were *so* excited and they did a perfect job. We got our biggest applause after their song. So when we were coming down the steps off the stage, I told them they caused all the applause.

Of all the people in the world, there at the bottom of the steps was Cliff Clawhammer, who does The Kiddie Show on Channel 9 every Saturday morning from 10:00 to 10:30. He plays the banjo and sings a little song at the end of every show. He looked just like on TV except older too—like Bob Ross. I guess TV does that to you. He looked about sixty, whereas on television, about fifty.

"Let me shake your hand, Miss," he says to Mary Faye at the bottom of the stairs. "And yours too," he says to Norris.

"Ain't you Cliff Clawhammer?" shouts Norris.

"That's right. On television, anyway." He tipped his cowboy hat—it was felt and making him sweat—and shook Charles's hand and said he enjoyed the music. He had on a shiny red shirt and a black western tie.

"What's your name, honey?" he asked Mary Faye.

"Mary Faye Bell."

"And yours?"

"Norris Bell. I seen you on television."

"Well, keep watching. You all excuse me. They want me to sing a few songs after this group and I've got to tune up.

I thought he seemed a little tipsy, but I figured it must be my imagination, and didn't think nothing else about it.

I went over to where the Golden Agers were. They were all very complimentary about our singing. I made Mary Faye and Norris go along and meet them all, and say thank you to the compliments—which they do without my help: Mama has seen to that. The Golden Agers were all having a good time and doing okay so we put our lawn chairs and blanket down front with Mama and Daddy, got settled and listened to the rest of Cliff Claw hammer's songs: "Peach Pickin' Time in Georgia" and "Curly Headed Baby," which he dedicated to Mary Faye and Norris: "This here's for two future award winning country singers: Norris and Mary Faye Bell."

Norris and Mary Faye were excited to death.

When he came down off stage he went up and sat with the Golden Agers and talked to them for about half an hour. Norris and Mary Faye went over and listened. I would have gone too, but Charles didn't want to.

But here's what happened late in the afternoon. At 3:30 Aunt Flossie loaded up the Golden Agers. Two had already left with somebody in their family, and one had been dropped off at home after the cannon firing, so Aunt Flossie thanked us and told us we could stay if we wanted, that there was plenty of room to take everybody home without us. So we decided to stay. At about four, Mama and Daddy left, but Mary Faye and Norris stayed to ride back with us.

At about 5:00, during a break, me, Charles, Mary Faye, and Norris decided to walk up the hill to the parking area where three guys were playing guitars and fiddle. Charles took his banjo and joined right in—sounding good.

I hadn't seen Cliff Clawhammer since after lunch. All of a sudden I saw him and this woman coming from the stage area, walking up the hill toward us. She's about fifty and is walking beside him and for some reason she's wearing this formal black dress and black high heel shoes. You could tell her hair was dyed because her face skin looked like it definitely would not have black hair—and she's wearing high heel shoes of all things, and all of a sudden it looks like this yellow page from the phone book floats down out of her mouth. Then another one. Well, it's of all things—I hate to even say this—vomit. She's not even stopping walking—just bending over a little, like she's too proud to stop, and all the while not getting a speck on her dress. It was like she knew just exactly how far to bend over while she walked.

And Cliff, he's sort of stumbling along, talking to her, and I realize they're both drunk and headed toward the portable outhouse not far from us.

Charles and the three boys were going strong: playing "Little Maggie."

Norris says, "Here comes Cliff Clawhammer!" and him and Mary Faye start toward him and the woman.

"Mary Faye, you and Norris get back here," I said. They could tell I meant business.

Mr. Clawhammer and the woman walk right past us like they don't even see us and he's saying, "Go ahead and puke, Alice. Don't be so 'g. d.' proud. Go ahead and puke."

I couldn't believe my ears. He really was cussing like that. Cliff Clawhammer. Talking like that to a woman. She won't his wife because she didn't have on a wedding ring. She was in a trance, and he was wobbling along beside her with his eyebrows pulling up his eyelids like he was trying to stay awake.

He led her over to the bathroom, then waited for her, then they walked back by us without speaking, him stumbling, with his red shirt tail all out in back, and her walking with her head up like she's walking down a aisle.

It was a disgrace.

I had hoped it wouldn't come up on the way home, but it did.

Norris and Mary Faye were sitting in the back seat.

"Why was Cliff Clawhammer's wife sick?" said Norris.

"She was drunk," said Mary Faye.

"How do you know?" said Norris.

"You could tell."

"Could not."

"You all be quiet," I said. "They were drunk, Norris. It's a sad fact, but they were."

"*She* was drunk?" asked Norris.

"Yes, I think so."

"I didn't know women got drunk."

"Anybody can get drunk," says Mary Faye. "Miss Peabody said some children in the ghetto get drunk because of their lifestyle."

"Sometimes people want to escape things," said Charles.

"That does not make it right," I said. "You're sounding like psychology."

"Well. . . ."

"Is it a sin for a woman to get drunk?" asked Norris.

"It's a sin for anybody," said Mary Faye. "Mama said it was a sin when Uncle Nate got drunk. I'm not going to ever touch one drop of liquor or beer or anything else. I promised."

I remembered. I'd promised too. I must have been about five. I can't believe I forgot. But the little bit of wine I'd drunk didn't seem to count

148

somehow. Then I wondered if maybe it had to count. Then I figured it didn't.

"Promised who?" said Charles.

"Mama," me and Mary Faye said together.

"I promised too," said Norris, "because it's a sin. I promised to try not to sin."

"She said not to *do* it," said Mary Faye. "Not just 'try' not to."

"She said to *try* not to sin," said Norris. "That Jesus would forgive you if you did it and were sorry and asked him to."

"She said to *not* sin."

"*Try* not to."

"Wait a minute," said Charles. "What are some other sins?"

"Don't you know?" said Norris.

"Well, I've got my own ideas," said Charles.

"Lying and stealing and cheating are the others. You'd *better* know what they are."

"What about gossip?" said Charles. "Ever talk about that?"

"I don't think that's one of the sins," said Norris.

"Oh, well," said Charles, "maybe we can talk about it sometime."

I wasn't sure what he was getting at, exactly.

For the rest of the way home I tried to explain to Mary Faye and Norris as best I could how drinking could ruin your life, how Uncle Nate had missed opportunities to live a full Christian

149

life because of alcohol and how people sometimes have to choose the narrow path or the wide path and the narrow path is full of thorns.

Then I got the narrow path and wide path backwards because somehow I thought Uncle Nate was taking the narrow path instead of the wide path. But it's just the opposite.

At church, Sunday, Aunt Flossie said it had been one of the best Golden Agers' days ever. Monday night about a minute of the cannon firing was on Channel 9 news. It showed all the Golden Agers standing watching and then Bob Ross talking to Mr. Earls and Aunt Flossie. You could hear "Salt Creek" in the background and there was a quick glimpse of me and Charles. And Aunt Flossie looked real good. Right at the very end, when Bob Ross finished talking to Aunt Flossie, you heard in the background: *"Birdie,* go get the—"; then it cut off.

I called up Aunt Flossie to see if she'd seen it. We'd been talking about how Mr. Earls hollered *"Birdie"* this and *"Birdie"* that. We thought it was funny it got on television. We said maybe it would be preserved forever.

Tuesday, I stopped by Aunt Flossie's and she was sewing. All of a sudden she said, *"Birdie,* hand me them scissors."

3

ONE OF THE ODDEST THINGS IN THE WORLD
has happened to Madora Bryant's oldest sister,
Jessie Faye. She and Richard, her husband,
found out they couldn't have any babies. Mama
heard he was the cause and Aunt Naomi heard
she was the cause. I asked Madora and she said
she didn't know but that Jessie Faye wouldn't
talk about it, so I haven't mentioned it to
anybody else. I figure if Jessie Faye wants to
keep it quiet then we all ought to respect that.

Well, they up and adopted a baby boy. Which I
think is all right. God might not want you to have
any babies of your own blood. That don't mean
it's not all right to have one that's been
abandoned.

They didn't have any problems adopting since
they'd both been to college, except it took over
two years. *But.* It turns out that the baby is half
colored. He looks that way anyway. Everybody
says so.

I don't think anybody has necessarily been
done any harm, unless he turns on Jessie Faye
and Richard. And off and on the coloreds get in
the habit of burning down their own houses. The
only other harm is that people notice and talk
which could hurt Richard and Jessie Faye's
feelings, or the little boy's. I'm not going to

mention it because you never know when something might happen to you that other people could talk about.

Charles gets blue in the face on this one: the whole segregation thing, as I said. He says they are burning down unfair landlords' houses, not their own houses, but I say all you've got to do is read the paper to find out they're burning down their own houses and shops right there in their own neighborhoods and as soon as they start, they steal a TV set out of a display window before it gets burned. I'm sure it has something to do with their forefathers having those bonfires in Africa.

The Indians are the same way—they still have things like that left in their blood; it's just a matter of time for them to outgrow it. I'll bet scientists will discover all that one day. Uncle Newton used to say he wished the Indians and the niggers would get in a war and that any American who could get that war started deserved the medal of honor. He was just kidding though. At least I think he was just kidding. I think we're all Americans. But the rest have got to get used to the melting pot like the whites have. You can't stay outside the melting pot and still be a true American.

Yesterday, when we had Christmas dinner over at Aunt Naomi's, it happened. We always have Christmas dinner at her house—early in

December, to avoid the rush. We had eaten dinner and exchanged presents (we draw names in November—you're not supposed to spend over two dollars. Aunt Flossie said we ought to raise it to three but that got voted down).

Now I don't mind Charles having odd opinions about segregation so much as I do the fact that he has to announce it to the family.

Here's what happened. It was Uncle Nate who brought the whole thing up. Me, Charles, Mary Faye, and Norris were sitting on the living room couch and Uncle Nate and Uncle Norris—who little Norris was named after—were sitting across the room. Uncle Norris is Mama's brother from Charlotte. Other people were in and out. Uncle Nate looks at us and says, "Have you all seen Jessie Faye Burton's boy?" He was eating a piece of chess pie as big as the Baptist Hymnal—in a plate on his knees.

"Yes," I said. I have never brought the subject up, but that baby has got to looking more and more like a little high-yellow. I don't know what the right name is: octagon or something. He looked as normal as he could as a baby. I saw him. But he was baldheaded then. Now his hair is as kinky as . . . well, as a nigger's.

Charles has done told me that if one of our children ever says "nigger" he's going to slap him across the room. I can't see that. Now I do think a person shouldn't say "nigger" *to* a nigger—unless maybe the nigger acts like one.

And I think if a person like Charles is offended easily, you should probably say "blacks." They're entitled to their own opinion.

Well, after I'd said yes I'd seen Jessie Faye's boy, Uncle Nate said, "He looks like a nigger, don't he?" He was eating his chess pie with a spoon.

I said, "He does to me." Right away I worried about what Charles was thinking, or what he was going to say.

What he said was, "What difference does that make?"

Uncle Nate and Uncle Norris looked at Charles like his nose had just fell off. Then Uncle Nate says, "What *difference* does it make?"

"That's right," says Charles. "What difference does it make?"

"Do you want a nigger youngin'?" says Uncle Nate. "Cause if you do, you married into the wrong family." He looked at Uncle Norris, then got up to carry his plate and spoon back to the kitchen.

"I don't think skin color makes any difference," says Charles.

"It makes you a nigger," says little Norris.

"Be quiet," I said. "Go get me some tea. Here, take this glass."

I thought of all the years the colored people around Bethel and Listre had lived in real low conditions and had never amounted to anything and I figured if Charles thought skin color didn't make a difference then he must be blind.

Uncle Nate, heading toward the kitchen, stopped, turned around, came back and sat down still holding his plate and spoon. He looked back and forth between Charles and Uncle Norris and then glanced at me like he couldn't believe what Charles just said. I was thinking, "Oh *no*."

"The difference it makes . . . the difference it makes," said Uncle Nate, "is that it makes you a white man or a nigger. That's the difference it makes."

"That's what Norris said," said Mary Faye.

"Stay out of this, Mary Faye," I said. "Why don't you go outside and play?"

"I don't want to."

"I mean any real difference," says Charles to Uncle Nate.

"Do you see any difference between a rabbit and a coon?" says Uncle Nate. His face was getting red and I could see tiny red blood vessels in his cheeks.

"Yes—but not between a black rabbit and a white rabbit," says Charles, "and that's the *real* issue." He was up on the front edge of the couch.

Daddy came to the living room door, but went back to the kitchen.

I could not figure what all these animals had to do with anything. Anybody knows a white rabbit and a black rabbit wouldn't mind marrying if they could, but that white people and colored people do mind marrying. That right there is difference enough for me. If it was natural for white and colored folks to marry then they would do it. God made us all to do natural things. Just look out your window at all the birds and animals doing natural things. That's what God made them to do: natural things. That's why dogs are so happy—they do natural dog things. You never see a dog doing something God didn't intend him to do. You never see a dog doing a cat thing or a bird thing. Never.

Now when you look out that window you don't see colored people and white people getting married. That's very simple because God didn't make that as one of the natural things for people in the world to do. If I married a colored man something inside me would say, "Raney, you are doing a very unnatural thing." Course I would never do that anyway. But I mean if I did. It's as plain as the nose on your face and some of these ideas of Charles's must come from a part of his brain which has never known about the natural and unnatural things God has intended for us to do.

"The difference between a black rabbit and a white rabbit," said Uncle Nate, "is their color. But the difference between a white man and a nigger is smell, lips, nose, hair, clothes, and laziness, and if you don't know that then you ain't been on the street lately."

Charles stood up and walked right out. Just stood up and walked out. It embarrassed me to death.

So there I was sitting next to an empty spot on the couch and Uncle Nate, Uncle Norris, and Mary Sue and Fred Toggert, who'd just that minute, before the argument ended, come in from down the road, all looking at me and each other like somebody had slapped a preacher. So I sat up straight and said I hoped they wouldn't hold it against Charles—that he had some unusual ideas about colored people, that his daddy was a college professor, but that underneath he had one of the best hearts in the world—I knew—and that his unusual ideas came from being raised sheltered-like. I was embarrassed to death—felt like I was making a speech. Nobody said anything. Uncle Nate stood up and walked out, headed to the kitchen, carrying his plate and spoon in his hand.

So last night at home I tried to explain to Charles about how embarrassed I'd been, but he wouldn't speak! Said we'd talk about it later and walked off into the kitchen closing every door behind him.

I went to bed.

The vent.

"You wouldn't believe it, Johnny. . . . No, oh

no, you wouldn't believe it. We were talking about *rabbits*. . . . Never mind."

Then the furnace came on and I couldn't hear a thing.

When the furnace went back off, Charles was asking Johnny, of all things, if he'd ever had any fried okra. He went on about how good it was! (Mama freezes it, thaws it, flours it, then fries it. She brought some to the Christmas dinner. I don't think it's that good after it's frozen.)

I figured I would explain to Charles about being able to hear through the vent as soon as he hung up.

But I forgot, because while I was laying there I got to thinking about Charles being outnumbered and that maybe Johnny Dobbs really was one of his best friends—that something traumatic in the army had *caused* them to be good friends.

If I had lived back in Bible times as a Hebrew and had been good friends with an Egyptian, then think of the problems that would have come out of that. Or what if I'd been friends with somebody who had leprosy: everybody back then hated people with leprosy. If I had married into a family—sort of like Charles has—who didn't understand that you *could* be friends with an Egyptian or a leopard, then the problems—all in all—would have been worse.

4

UNCLE NEWTON DIED AT HOME LAST FRIDAY. On Saturday night before the funeral on Sunday, we went over to Aunt Minnie's with Mama, sat for awhile, and then took Aunt Minnie and Louise, their daughter, up to the funeral home. The family was scheduled to be there from seven to nine.

I had a hard time talking Charles into going with us. I told him I'd cook him some brownies and would he please at least pay respect where respect was due and that I'd feel abandoned up there at the funeral home without him. He kept saying it was all primitive. I wondered what in the world they do with all his folks when they die—cremint them? They're doing that in some of the bigger cities now. What I can't understand is: that is what the Indians used to do to settlers—tie them to a pole and cremint them.

When we got to Aunt Minnie's, she went all to pieces. Louise was back in her bedroom and hadn't come out more than twice, so Aunt Minnie said. To eat, I imagine—not counting the times she went to the bathroom. Louise is seventeen, does ballet, and dates a college boy.

While Aunt Minnie was crying, she told Charles that he had always been one of Uncle Newton's favorite nephews. I'm afraid that wasn't quite the truth—Aunt Minnie must have been delirious. The only times Uncle Newton and Charles saw each other was the time me and Charles visited him right before we got married, and then the one time about two weeks ago. Both times Uncle Newton asked Charles how many colored people were at the college and Charles—of course—complained on the way home, both times, about Uncle Newton being a racist, which of course Uncle Newton is—was—not.

At about six-thirty we left Aunt Minnie's for the funeral home: Wayside, next to the Goodwill. Mary Faye and Norris were along and had been arguing since we left Mama's: first, about whether or not the army could arrest you for speeding, and then about how much money was in the world. Mama told them they'd have to hush if they wanted to go in and see Uncle Newton.

We walked up to the casket: me, Mama, Aunt Minnie, Louise, Mary Faye, Norris, and Mrs. Fuller. Mrs. Fuller is a neighbor of Aunt Flossie's. She's the assistant treasurer at the church and knows how much money everybody gives, so Mama says. She'll go to the funeral home for a night out. Nosy, but just as helpful as she can be. She takes in cats—and dips snuff. (If she's dipping in public, she'll spit into a handful of Kleenex.)

At the casket, Aunt Minnie and Louise went all

to pieces. The funeral home man—Kenneth Simmons's uncle, Mr. Simmons—was real supportive, just sort of standing there. Kenneth Simmons is a boy I used to date, and he worked there at the funeral home one summer—drove a hearse—and he told me about all the little things funeral home people do, like show caskets, and make all the arrangements, and things like that.

So Mr. Simmons tells Aunt Minnie that the funeral home can do anything she wants about changing the way Uncle Newton looks, his face or anything. She starts bawling again, poor thing, and asks Mr. Simmons to pin on Uncle Newton's Kiwanis pin which she gets out of her pocketbook. He went over and pinned it right on.

I cried too. Aunt Minnie's and Uncle Newton's house was the first place I ever remember visiting, and Uncle Newton always gave me a piece of chewing gum after church. He was one of the kindest and quietest people in our whole family.

I turned around to grab for Charles's hand, and he was *not even there.* He was standing back there in the little waiting room reading the guest book! That's where he'd been the whole time.

I walked back, grabbed his arm, and said, "Charles, what's the matter with you? Uncle Newton looks real good. Come on. He looks just like he's asleep."

He was in one of those battleship grey caskets.

"I don't want to look at your Uncle Newton."

I couldn't imagine. "Charles," I whispered, "he's not just *my* Uncle Newton. He's your uncle too—by the act of marriage. Are you deserting him because he's dead?"

Charles was as stiff as a statue.

"Okay, he's my uncle too," he says. "I'd rather remember him the way he was. I have absolutely no need or desire to view a corpse."

About that time Mama comes up with Norris and Mary Faye. "Don't he look good?" she says. "Charles, did you look in on him?"

"Look *in* on him?" says Charles.

"Did you see him?"

"No, I didn't."

"Why not, son? You don't want to pay your respects?"

"It's not a matter of respect," Charles says. "I paid him my respects when he was alive."

I didn't want to make the argument any worse, but as far as I'm concerned, Charles paid mighty few respects when Uncle Newton was alive. So I said, "What kind of respects did you ever pay to Uncle Newton?"

"I visited him," said Charles. "Kept him posted on integration."

Can you believe that? That's all Charles could think up to say after the whole life Uncle Newton led as a delivery man and a Christian.

Mama says, "Would you do it for Minnie and

Louise, son? I know it'd make them feel better."

Charles says, "It would make *you* feel better, Mrs. Bell. Because you—"

Mr. Simmons steps up and says in this real low voice, "Is there anything wrong? Something I can do?"

Mama and me were flabbergasted. Charles, of course, has read some articles which talk about the funeral home business being a "racket"—he's talked about it—so what he ups and says just about knocked out the bottom of my world, given the condition I was in anyway. He says, "Mr. Simmons, do you realize that some families can't afford a two thousand dollar funeral? Do you realize that by displaying those expensive caskets the way you do, you make people feel guilty if they don't get one? Do you realize that?"

Mr. Simmons stayed composed. "We—"

"Why don't you display the cheaper caskets for people to decide on—especially poor folks?"

"We believe that—"

"I know what you believe. I've read about what you believe. You believe you can squeeze two thousand dollars from some grieving widow who can't think straight—rather than explain to her that a funeral does not *have* to be so damned expensive. Your 'profession' has carried this whole business to the extreme. And I can't believe you people stand up there in your casket display room and talk about how one vault is guaranteed not to leak within fifty years and another within one hundred years and that kind of garbage. I'm sorry. It just burns me up."

And Charles walked straight out to the car.

Mr. Simmons says, still in his low voice, "Death affects people in many ways. I'm sure Charles will feel better in a day or two. Don't you all worry about it one bit."

I was so embarrassed. I almost said, "That man is not my husband." But I didn't.

It just doesn't make sense that something so connected to decency, like a funeral, could get Charles so riled up. I know it's those articles he's been reading. One of the drawbacks of being well read like Charles is that sometimes he comes across something in a normally good magazine which got in there by mistake, written by some quirk. I think sometimes Charles don't think for himself.

What really hurts deep down is I don't know if Charles will want to look at Mama and Daddy at their funerals. And, of course, if anything ever happened to me: I just can't bear the thought of me laying up there in a casket in the funeral home—dead—while Charles stands in the waiting room, mouthing off to the funeral director—never having looked on my body.

Last Tuesday afternoon I took Mama some eggs—after I got my hair done—and we talked about Charles. I was expecting her to bring up something about how he behaved at the funeral home.

"Sugar," Mama says, "I want to ask you a question. Why does Charles sit so quiet when we eat Sunday dinner? I get the feeling I don't know him yet. And the way he acted at Newton's funeral. Where in the world did that come from?"

"Well, Mama, you got to understand something about Charles's background. The whole way he grew up affected him."

"Well, honey, there comes a time when a person has to learn how to get along with other people, how to be a little outgoing. And I don't mind a person disagreeing with me like Charles has a few times, but I just feel like he could show a little more interest in me and your daddy. Course him and Thurman do seem to get along pretty well."

"He's learning, Mama. It takes time. Sometimes his background experience don't tell him nothing while mine tells me exactly what to do. Charles got a lot of book learning and that's been good to him in some ways. He's got a good job at the library and he knows about books whereas I grew up around people. And he's a real good musician, and we love the same kind of music, and he gets along with people, and—"

"Honey, you had plenty of books when you was growing up."

"I know it, Mama, but I'm talking about books on philosophy and astrology and things like that."

"Well, I don't understand how a person's background can make a person sit at the dinner table and not hardly say one word to another person throughout an entire Sunday dinner."

"Mama, I just think it might take you some time to get to know Charles. He's trying. Honest."

While we talked I heard this voice inside me saying, "Raney, Charles don't like your mama and you know it."

Now what I want to know is how can a woman like me, or any woman for that matter, say to her own mama, "Mama, my husband don't like you"?

But on the other hand, how can a woman like me, or any woman for that matter, say to her own husband, "Husband, my mama don't like you"?

5

I WENT TO THE MALL LAST THURSDAY FOR THE new year specials. When I got home and walked in the door, Charles was standing in the middle of the living room looking at me like I had a snake on my head.

"Charles, what's the matter?"

"Sit down for a minute."

I sat on the couch with my coat on, holding three shopping bags.

"Mr. Donaldson just called."

"What Mr. Donaldson?"

"Your next door neighbor in Bethel."

"What did he want?"

"Uncle Nate shot himself. This afternoon. He's still alive though—in County Hospital."

Everything in the room dropped away and all my strength faded. "Charles. What in the world? How?"

"With his pistol."

"Was it a accident?"

"Well, I don't know. I don't think so."

"Let me call Mama."

"She's probably at the hospital."

"Maybe Daddy's at home."

I stood up and walked to the phone. My legs were weak and my chest felt tight. Pictures of Uncle Nate were swimming through my head. Mr. Donaldson answered. He said Mama and Daddy were at the hospital. I was trying to think where in the world in the house it happened and if there was blood or whatever, so I asked if there was anything to clean up. Mr. Donaldson said everything was okay, that there won't anything to clean up, and that Uncle Nate must have gone crazy with his nerves and asthma being so bad. He said Mama had carried him up to the VA hospital that morning and that they wouldn't let him in and he came home and tried to shoot himself in the back of the head with a pistol and ended up shooting himself in the neck, and then he walked out on the front porch and fell into the shrubs and nobody knew about it until Mama came home from Nell Howard's and saw him when she started up the front steps.

My chest tightened up more and I felt like I was in a trance. All I could see was Uncle Nate's face with his hair slicked back and the way he looked with his white shirt and coat on when he was getting ready to go to Sunday School.

Me and Charles drove to the County Hospital and walked into the emergency room waiting area. The lights seemed too bright. Mama and Daddy and Aunt Flossi were standing with the doctor. "How do you do. I'm Dr. Scarborough," he said. He was tall, skinny, young, bald-headed, and wearing wire rimmed glasses. I didn't like him. Mama and Aunt Flossie looked scared to death.

I thought about Dr. Cisco, who set Norris's thumb. I wondered if there was a way Uncle Nate could get him for a doctor. At least he would know how to talk to us like a normal human being and make us feel better.

"I was just telling your folks," said the doctor to me, "that Mr. Purvis has a less than fifty percent chance of making it through the night. The bullet is lodged near the juncture of his brain and spinal column in the upper neck area. We're trying to stop the bleeding as best we can. If he stabilizes we'll try to remove the bullet. It'll be a while before we know whether or not we can do that."

"He's always been strong," said Mama.

"We'll be moving him to intensive care in an hour or so," said the doctor. "If you'd like to stay, the intensive care waiting room is a little more comfortable than here. I need to be running along now," He walked off.

"I like him," Mama said. "He's a specialist. One of the best, said one of the nurses. I asked her about him." So I didn't say anything about Dr. Cisco.

Things jumped around in my head. I saw Uncle Nate standing in the living room door at home on Sunday afternoons after he'd walk down the hall from his room to watch the ballgame with Daddy. I saw him standing at the picture window looking out while he combed his hair.

We got settled in the intensive care waiting room. There was a TV in there and it was on a game show and the color was awful—green and pink—and I wondered why anybody was watching it—how somebody could sit there and watch a game show while their uncle or aunt or mother or father was sick in intensive care.

Mama started telling me and Charles what happened:

"He'd stopped taking them drugs about two days ago. He said he wouldn't start back if it killed him. If he took them he couldn't stay awake and if he didn't take them, he couldn't sleep."

"What was he taking?" Charles asked.

"Librium and thorosene or something."

"Where did he get that?"

"Sedgwick Drugs—Tillman Sedgwick."

"He didn't have a prescription?"

"From 1960, '61, I think."

"My God," says Charles.

"He'd been taking them a long time to stay off liquor."

"But . . ." says Charles.

"So," says Mama, "he hadn't slept hardly none for three or four nights—up and down, up and down, and having asthma attacks and taking his spray for that. This morning he wanted to know if I could take him up to the VA hospital, that he had to get some help. And you know Nate—he won't ask nobody for help. So I took him. He was as nervous as he could be. Lord knows I didn't know what all this was coming to. His nerves were tore all to pieces. He couldn't stop pulling at his ear—like this. He's been doing that for months now.

"We had to wait for two hours. Then this young doctor comes out—real young fellow—I didn't even know he was a doctor. He didn't introduce

170

hisself or nothing—just started in telling Nate he had reviewed his record and that he was sorry but they couldn't treat him because they didn't handle something or other. He didn't even look at me. Nate told him he had to have some help. That *something* had to be done. Anything, but *something*. He was in worse shape than I've ever seen him. He was so nervous he didn't know what to do. So I asked the doctor couldn't he see that Nate needed help—couldn't he see he was a sick man, a sick man and a veteran, and that we were in a veterans' hospital and why in the *world* couldn't the government help its veterans if it could help every fourteen year old nigger girl in the country that had a bastard baby. He said he won't no politician and he was sorry but that we would have to *leave*. I looked at his name tag— Boyd was his name—and told him my congressman would hear about him and to send me to his boss right that minute. Nate was crying. Dr. Boyd says, 'Mr. Purvis, do you want to see Dr. Blotner?' And Nate looks up and says Yes. So Dr. Boyd gets this Dr. Blotner who says there is absolutely nothing he can do, he is very sorry—that there is nothing the VA hospital can do for Nate, that he would be happy to give us a complaint form, but that their priorities didn't allow them to treat drug related problems and that—of all things—I should take Nate to a psychiatric.

"So we drove on back home and I told Nate that he'd just have to rely on the Lord and that I'd done everything I could for years and years, and that I'd tried to tell him all along what it was coming to—that you can't go against the Lord's word for year after year and not expect any consequences.

"Well, I'd told Nell that I'd bring her some frozen squash and Lord it's not but three houses away and I never heard a thing. He took the gun out of that drawer he keeps it in, I reckon. Thank goodness Mary Faye and Norris won't there."

"Could it have been an accident?" Charles asked.

"Oh, no. No, it won't a accident. I asked him what happened while he was laying there in the shrubs—before I saw the blood. I couldn't imagine. Then I saw the blood pooling out under his neck in the dirt. He was looking up at me. The blood looked like molasses. I said, 'What happened, Nate?!' And he said, 'I shot myself. To get it over with.' He looked like he tried to lean up, then his eyes closed and his head dropped down in the dirt. I told him that we loved him and that he shouldn't have done that. I grabbed him around the shoulders to try to get him up on the porch. Then I saw how much blood there was and it all struck me like lightning. I stood up and started screaming for help and, oh Lord. . . ."

The doctor came in and said Uncle Nate was

resting as comfortable as possible and that he was in shock and couldn't have any visitors— that somebody would let us know if there was any change. We tried to decide who could stay and who could go home for awhile. Mama wanted to stay, so I said I'd stay with her. Aunt Naomi had picked up Mary Faye and Norris from school and was staying with them at home. Daddy, Aunt Flossie, and Charles stayed for about three hours and then left to get something to eat, and to explain to Mary Faye and Norris. At first we couldn't decide what to tell them but we finally settled on the truth. Mama said they weren't old enough but then she agreed.

Mama and me waited in the intensive care waiting room. At about seven o'clock the doctor came in and said Uncle Nate was in a coma. At eight he came back and said Uncle Nate had died about ten minutes before, suddenly—that his heart just stopped.

My arms felt numb, and I couldn't cry. I was too tired, I think. Mama burst into crying and said it was all her fault. Then I burst into crying. Then I wondered why they hadn't let us in to see him before he died. Didn't they know we'd want to see him?

I called Wayside Funeral Home from this little office which the doctor took us to. I asked for Mr. Simmons. He came on the phone and said he'd take care of everything but wondered if there was going to be an autopsy. I asked the doctor and he asked Mama and she said no.

Mama wanted to see him. I didn't. I just didn't think I could. I decided I'd wait until the funeral. The doctor took Mama in Uncle Nate's room and I heard her crying. There were all sorts of people in there. I stared at two swinging doors down the hall. People came in and out.

Two or three times during the drive home—I drove—Mama said that she had failed, that she should have been more patient and that Uncle Nate had never had nobody and always had bad luck and was a good man at heart. I tried to tell her it won't her fault. She wouldn't listen.

This was all Thursday. Right away everybody started bringing food to the house. Friday, Uncle Norris came from Charlotte. Uncle Nate didn't have any living relatives except Mama and Aunt Flossie and Uncle Norris. There had been his wife, but she died in 1957 after they got their divorce in 1952. They got married in 1951.

Everybody wanted to know what happened and Mama told the story over and over. "What in the world happened, Doris?" And "Why in the world do you suppose he did it, Doris?" Mama told it over and over about how he had come home from the war, burned like he was, and with his bad lungs and having those asthma attacks and having to sit still for four or five hours and not able to find a job on account of it, and how she

174

had tried to take care of him all these years and bring him to Christ and that he had finally been saved (she prayed and hoped) in December of '71 and cut back on his drinking but hadn't been able to quit completely and that he had to take drugs to help keep off liquor.

Mr. Brooks, one of the church deacons, came over Friday afternoon and said he had read that the family requested that no flowers be sent. (Uncle Nate liked that Carter family song: "Give me the roses while I live; trying to cheer me on. Useless are flowers that you give after the soul is gone." And Mama said he wrote down about his funeral one time and showed it to her and it said no flowers, contributions to the Elon Boys' Home instead.) So Mr. Brooks is wearing his suit—he always wears it—and he's sitting in the living room asking people if they'd like to make a remembrance donation to the Missionary Building Fund, since it had been requested that no flowers be sent. (Next day, Mrs. Fuller said he said something about the unfortunate truth that people who committed suicide were breaking the ten commandments. I can't imagine where his heart is.) I've never been able to like Mr. Brooks: he's always quoting scripture and getting mad at people and *places:* like I've heard him run down New York, and Paris, and Chapel Hill. There's bound to be good and bad people in those places, just like anywhere else. I know if Jesus had been like Mr. Brooks he certainly would have had a hard time finding disciples who would *like* him. The twelve disciples *had* to like Jesus or they wouldn't have stuck with him like they did, through thick and thin. People say Mr. Brooks knows the Bible better than most preachers. I just can't ever feel any heart about him. When his heart seems to peep through, it feels like a lie. I know it's wrong to judge him like that but sometimes I can't help it.

I said, and I took a deep breath and closed my eyes, "Mr. Brooks, Uncle Nate made it clear that he wanted donations to go to the Elon Boys' Home." I felt like I had to say it for Uncle Nate—because he would have said it.

"We give to the Boys' Home—provide building funds every other year," says Mr. Brooks, "so it's the same thing."

"Well," I says, "I don't think it is the same thing. I don't think—"

"Raney, let's let these people decide for themselves. I think they can—"

"My Uncle Nate is the one who has already decided, Mr. Brooks. It's his place to make this decision, not these people's or anybody else's, or yours. He's the one who died and had the right to say what's to be done in the area of flowers and donations. *Everybody,*" I said. *"Everybody please come in here. I have an announcement."* We were in the living room. I had to get this straightened out. And deep down I know what Uncle Nate thought of Mr. Brooks. What most people think of Mr. Brooks. He'll sit in church and nod his head when he approves and disapproves—like the Pharisees Jesus talked about, showing themselves in church. Two Sundays ago I was sitting behind him and he nodded his disapproval at a real cute skit two girls did right before the service. The very idea: as if the final word resided in him. Then right after that when they made the announcement that three boys were going to read the New Testament from start to finish on the next Saturday, he nodded his *approval*. I think he had it backwards. Those boys ought to be out mowing some old people's grass. You never heard of Jesus standing around all day reading out loud when he could be doing something for somebody who needed help.

People came in from the kitchen and stood in the doorways and all around. There was already a bunch of people sitting in the living room. I was nervous, but I was mad. "You all," I said, "Uncle Nate asked, and the newspaper says, that donations go to the Elon Boys' Home—no flowers. And I just wanted to repeat that because I think Uncle Nate's wishes should be followed." I was hoping that's all I would have to say. That it would be over with that.

Mrs. Fuller—of course—asks, "What about

the Missionary Building Fund?" She has a God-given knack.

"I don't think so," I said. "I'm sorry, but I really don't think so. I mean that was not included in what Uncle Nate told me and Mama. If the Boys' Home wants to donate to the Building Fund, that's fine."

There was this pause. Mr. Brooks was sitting there in front of the picture window with it getting dark outside and Mama's *Gone With the Wind* lamp lit over his shoulder. He didn't say anything, thank goodness; he just got up and walked out, mad I guess, and it didn't bother me one iota. Not one bit. I was tore all to pieces anyway and here he comes collecting money, of all things, over somebody's dead body.

Daddy was shook up through the whole thing. He mostly sat around not saying anything. Not laughing. Some people laugh and talk like the dead person hasn't died. But Daddy just sat like somebody had slapped him, and mother told about what had happened over and over and all about how she had tried through the years to get Uncle Nate straight and that she guessed she had failed.

That night we all went to the funeral home. I was worried that Charles would make a scene like with Uncle Newton but he didn't. He even walked up to the casket and looked at Uncle Nate, who looked like he was asleep. His coloring was real good, in spite of what had happened.

It was all a shock. There was this giant black hole in my life. And it couldn't all hit me at once. It was like a hourglass was holding things back.

When we'd been back from the funeral home about thirty minutes, Mary Faye came over and sat down beside me on the couch and said she thought Uncle Nate must have been real worried about things to shoot himself. I agreed. Charles came over and sat beside me and asked me where Norris was. I said I didn't know.

"Let's take him and Mary Faye for a ride to Hardee's and see how they're doing."

I hadn't even thought about Mary Faye and Norris. Charles thinks about things like that sometimes and I'm so thankful he's that way. I know he'll be a good father because of it.

Norris was in the kitchen eating apple pie. The food was mounting up.

On the way to Hardee's, Charles asked them how they were feeling about it all. They said they were sad. Mary Faye said she kept seeing Uncle Nate's face in her mind. Norris said that Jimmy Pope said Uncle Nate should have shot himself in the temple if he wanted to do it right, and Norris said he told Jimmy that if he didn't have something good to say to shut up. I told him that's exactly what he should have said.

While we were at Hardee's, Norris asked us

why people commit suicide and Charles explained about not having anything to hope for and having your body hurt real bad. He explained it all. I didn't have to explain much. He got it just about right. I'm glad we gave them some attention. I think they needed it.

Saturday, the funeral home men drove up the driveway in the big silver gray cars. Mr. Simmons came in the back door and made a little speech about what everybody was supposed to do. Charles didn't say a word.

Somebody had thrown a Coke-a-Cola can in the yard out by the driveway, so before we got in the cars, we had to wait for Mama to pick it up and put it in the trash around back. I'm glad there weren't fifteen or twenty. The sky looked like snow and it was freezing cold.

The funeral was about what you'd expect, and was short, thank goodness. I couldn't rid my mind of Uncle Nate's face and his starched white shirts with the collar open.

In his message, Preacher Gordon said that Uncle Nate was one of the last casualties of World War II. I hadn't thought about it that way.

6

ON WEDNESDAY NIGHT, ELEVEN DAYS AFTER the funeral, just after we watched this TV show about a little girl's mother committing suicide, Charles says he thinks that under different circumstances Uncle Nate might not have committed suicide.

"What do you mean by that?" I said.

"Raney, he was very depressed. He needed psychiatric help. But no one in the family seemed to care whether he got it or not."

"Charles, I don't think Uncle Nate needed a psychiatric."

"Psychologist, or psychiatrist, is what you mean."

"Well, whatever. He was not mentally ill."

"Do you think he was depressed?"

"Well, I don't know."

"He was, Raney. Take my word for it. He was. And he was compulsive-obsessive. And *severely* depressed." Charles started to the kitchen. I followed him.

"*You're* in the family. Why didn't you do something?" I said.

"There's no way—you know how much weight my suggestions carry."

"Charles, you think that just because Uncle Nate got water at the same time every day there

181

was something wrong with him. I've heard you talk about that. I don't see it that way. You stick all these words on there and make it sound like he was some kind of cripple or something."

"He was. In the end, at least." Charles was getting out a can of pinto beans and a can of tomatoes to make chili for the next day.

"He wasn't a cripple," I said.

"Mentally. You know what I mean. Otherwise, he wouldn't have shot himself."

"Charles, you don't know that."

"Maybe not. But I do know he lived in a society which A) supplies mental health care for its citizens. There is a trained psychologist at the mental health clinic. Counseling services are offered for people with mental problems— depression included—in Hansen County. Your Uncle Nate was a citizen of Hansen County. Now B) your Uncle Nate was a member of a family which does not believe in mental health care. At least that much is true, it seems to me. It's nothing that can be helped."

I thought about Dr. Cisco. He knew all about these kinds of things. For sure he'd had training in psychology. And he wouldn't go list off "A, B, and C." He would know better than to tear into somebody who had done the best they could all their lives. Anybody would.

"Charles, I do not see how you can say that— how you've got the nerve to stand there and say that, after all the care my mama gave Uncle Nate over the years: after all the meals she cooked him, all the shirts she washed and pressed. . . ."

"That's just it, Raney. Who gives her the right to decide that's what your Uncle Nate needs—needed. Needed most."

"Charles, she's his sister—family. That's where her right came from. And he was her brother and she loved him enough to take care of him."

"Maybe that's just what he didn't need. Maybe what he needed was to take care of himself."

"Charles, he *couldn't*."

"Maybe he could. Have you ever thought about that?"

"Charles, don't be ridiculous. Maybe you should talk to Mama. Since you know so much. Maybe you should tell her all this. All she did, after all, was to look after her brother when he came out of the war, disabled, to help him as best she could. If she had your magnificent college education and knowledge about mental health then maybe she would have done different. But tell me this Charles: what would have happened to Uncle Nate if it hadn't been for Mama in the first place?"

"I don't know, Raney. And neither do you. That's what I was just talking about. Maybe he would have lived a longer and healthier and happier life than he did. Who knows?"

"Charles, why didn't *you* do something? You've got all the answers. *Now* you've got all the answers. Charles, I can't believe you're saying all this."

"Listen, Raney. I haven't said I have all the answers. I have tried to say things. God knows I've tried. And I give up. I couldn't care less. Your family is a brick wall. I couldn't care less. Why should I waste my time beating my head against a brick wall?"

He was standing there holding a pack of frozen hamburger to fix chili with, getting more and more intense. I was so mad I couldn't stand it. I knew it was coming. We had had a big argument every day—four days in a row. My cheeks got hot and my chest hurt and I felt ice water between my skin and rib cage. "Charles, I can't *live* with this! You think Mama murdered Uncle Nate!"

"No. No. Now, Raney, don't be ridiculous. It wasn't murder. It was a whole family's refusal to look for alternatives to a . . . a way of life. To read—to become educated about a problem staring you in the face. Given the self-righteousness of . . . of fundamental Christianity in this family, your Uncle Nate didn't have a chance."

Something snapped in my head, like a dam had broke loose, a dam that should have broke loose long before. I walked straight to the bedroom, got out the big suitcase and packed. It took ten minutes. I went straight to the phone and called Aunt Flossie and asked her if I could come to her house. Lord knows I couldn't call Mama with all she had on her. I felt determined and clear. Charles had just burned himself right out of my mind. There was nothing there but ashes. I did not have any idea where I would go after Aunt Flossie's. I could decide that later. I finished packing.

"Where are you going, Raney?" said Charles.

I was standing there holding the suitcase. I hated him. "You heard me talking to Aunt Flossie."

"I don't want you to leave. You don't have to leave over this. I was looking at the whole thing from a psychological, maybe socio-psychological, perspective. That's all."

"*Psychological?* Charles, that's not even something in this world. I will not live here and listen to you call my mama a murderer. It's that simple."

"Raney, I didn't call your mother a murderer. I only said that—"

"Charles, you son of a . . . you son of a. . . ." I couldn't hold back. I put the suitcase on the floor. "You son of a bitch. You stand there and try to weasel out of something you just said as clear as day. That's the way you are. You'll throw out all this garbage psychiatric crap and then say bad things about somebody's—your own wife's—mama, *and family,* all at the same time and then when somebody points it out, you try to, to, to, take it back, and then say you didn't. Anybody can come along after something like this has happened and look at it different and get real superior about what *should* have happened. You just think you know everything, Charles. Well, you don't know so much. You better know you're going to be eating that chili all by yourself, Charles. You better know that. You better know that." I had to cry.

"Raney, you need to settle down. We're all to blame, as a society, including me."

"Charles! You don't even . . . all you can do is *blame* somebody." I picked up the suitcase. "That's all you know how to do." I walked straight out of the house, got in the Chevrolet, and drove to Aunt Flossie's. I hated Charles. If he had all those things in him that he was saying I didn't want to live in the same house with him. I *couldn't.*

Aunt Flossie met me on the front porch. We went on in and she took me to her second bedroom.

"I was just getting out a towel and wash cloth. The bottom two drawers on that chest are empty and if that's not enough room, clean you out another drawer. There's space in the closet. Make yourself at home. You can stay here as long as you need to. Go and come as you please. If you want to talk I'll be happy to listen."

The telephone rang.

It was for me: Charles. "Raney, I want you to come back," he says.

"Charles. . . . Please leave me alone."

"Raney, I'm sorry. I think I was just upset about the whole thing. We need to talk about all this."

"Charles, I have my own family. I have my own family to talk to. Besides, what can I say to you, Charles, that would ever make one difference about one thing on earth."

This was serious business. My insides were tore all to pieces. My heart. I had this damp, clammy feeling because I was afraid it all might have gone too far, that we might not be able to climb back up out of the gully. I was pulled and pushed two different ways at one time and I didn't know which one to go with.

"Charles, I'm going to stay here at Aunt Flossie's until I get my mind straightened out and I'd appreciate it if you wouldn't call."

"Raney. . . ."

"Goodbye." I hung up. Then it struck me what the family was going to think. If there was any way to get out of that then I had to do it. I *couldn't*—just *couldn't*—let everybody find out my marriage was failing, but Lord knows, I had been so mad that all I could think about, all I could see in my head, was getting *out* of that house.

Maybe Charles would admit how wrong he was. Maybe he *would* listen. But I doubted it. Then I didn't doubt it a little bit. Then I doubted it again.

"Sit down and tell me all about it if you want to," says Aunt Flossie, coming back in the living room. Something flooded up from inside and I burst out in tears that came and came and came and kept coming and I couldn't do nothing about it and Aunt Flossie said to cry and keep crying all I wanted to, so I did.

I was finally able to explain everything—it poured and poured and poured out—about how the whole family was just starting to recover from a death and my own husband has to go make everything worse, throw everything off the deep end by accusing my mother of something she would never, never do in her life. And I told her about a few other arguments that had made me feel awful. But I tried to tell her that Charles might be doing the best he could.

Aunt Flossie didn't say anything much. She just patted me on the back and told me to cry all I wanted to.

7

I'T'S BEEN TWO DAYS NOW. I GO HOME AT around eight-thirty in the morning after Charles leaves for work. Then I come back to Aunt Flossie's before lunch in case Charles comes home for lunch. I suppose he still does. He always used to.

It's been the saddest thing. I don't get anything done when I'm home. Uncle Nate dying and then this with Charles has been worse than anything I've ever been through.

It's like the two main parts of my life, Charles and home, being struck through with sadness and hurt. And pure hate. I just can't understand what got into Charles. How he could say those things about Mama and my whole family. He seemed so intent on getting up on a white horse and saying all those things about Mama.

He's made a mistake sticking this psychology on people who're doing the best they can for each other. This psychology could give a good report on somebody who's *not* trying, but who's lucky; then on somebody who's *trying* it might turn up a bad report. There is no way to know who's trying unless you can look in their heart. Which we can't do.

Charles has a good heart. I know. He wouldn't have said all that psychology about Daddy or

Aunt Flossie. He'll sit around and talk to them and discuss things. But anybody else in the family don't have a chance and I know they all notice.

Sometimes I think life is a bed of rose thorns.

I started missing Charles today. Little things. One thing is he'll get excited about the newspaper, what's in the paper in the mornings, and I usually ask him a couple of questions about what he's shaking his head about or mumbling about. And you know Charles. He gets to going on about whatever it is, which is the way I learn about some of the news on TV. Plus those pajamas I kid him about. They've got sailboat steering wheels all over but I tell him they look like Cheerios or I ask him how his Cheerios feel, or what he's doing wearing Cheerios.

And I feel so alone.

Yesterday I left Charles a note asking him if he'd sent in this month's church money. This morning when I went home he had left a note saying he had. He also left me a cassette tape. And on the note he said he wanted to come by Aunt Flossie's to see me and maybe we could talk about seeing a psychiatric—a marriage counselor. He said he's just gone to see one and that if I didn't want to talk it over with him at lunch then to call him at work, otherwise he'd come by Aunt Flossie's. He said he missed me and was sorry it all happened, and that so much had seemed to come between us over the last few weeks, and that maybe we could just talk a little. I played the tape. It was Charles playing his banjo and singing:

I see the moon and the moon sees me.
The moon sees the one that I want to
      see.
God bless the moon and God bless me.
And God bless the one that I want to see.

It tore up my heart and I played it twice more. It tore up my heart all three times. It was so sweet and soft. (I wouldn't dare ever tell Charles, but his B string was very slightly flat.)

I talked it over with Aunt Flossie about us getting that kind of help. She seemed to think it's a good idea if the psychiatric has any sense. She agreed that something has to be done.

Charles came by at lunch. Before he came, Aunt Flossie had fixed us ham, cheese, and lettuce sandwiches and ice tea, brought it all in the living room and put it on the coffee table and then left to go shopping for some weather stripping—she said. I was watching when Charles turned in the driveway. He got out of the car with some kind of newspaper in his hand. He knocked and I let him in and we sat on the couch for a minute or two, not saying anything, just breathing, looking straight ahead at Aunt

Flossie's little roll top desk and the sandwiches on the coffee table.

"The sandwiches are for us," I said.

"Oh, good."

We picked up our sandwiches, took a bite, and sat there not saying anything, just breathing and chewing, looking straight ahead.

"Did you get my note?" said Charles.

"Yes, and the tape."

"Is it okay if I show you something here in the college newspaper?"

"Okay."

It was a newspaper article on marriage counseling at the Hansen County Mental Health Clinic.

"See," said Charles, "here it says these people 'have training in helping married couples find different ways to communicate and seek out sources of problems, including potentially destructive patterns of behavior.' I mean you don't have to be having any kind of mental problems, and this woman is really nice and I asked her about you coming along with me and she said she thought that was a very good idea, but only if you'd agree."

"A woman psychiatric?"

"Psychologist. Yes."

"I want to do *something,* Charles. All this has been so much and I feel so tired and some of those arguments and that last one just got me

192

down to the core and I don't know why all that happened. I feel so tired now. All that with Uncle Nate and now all this."

"I want to do something too, Raney. I . . . I . . ." Charles looked at me. His chin began to quiver and then his mouth and then his whole face got out of shape and he said, "I miss you."

My heart went to mush. I couldn't be mad. "I miss you too, Charles. And I miss your Cheerios pajamas."

He laughed and we hugged each other tight. He asked me if I still loved him and I said I did and he said he loved me too. How in the world things can be so one way and then so the other way I will never understand.

We agreed for me to come back home and I felt so relieved. I was so tired and I wanted to go home. I walked Charles out to the car and we talked for a few minutes out there. When I came back in, I noticed only one bite was gone from each one of our sandwiches. I was so hungry I sat down and ate both of them.

When Aunt Flossie got back she was really happy to hear the news and said she was glad we were going to try to work on things and not just let them get swept under the rug.

Driving home I tried to think about what was happening. I can understand hating Charles on the outside and loving him down in the core, but when you go through a bunch of arguments in a row and then through a short spell of hating your own husband all the way down in the core, then you've got to figure it out so that it won't get worse and worse. I'm willing to try anything—even a psychiatric. I figure a psychiatric might be able to explain to Charles at least some of what he did wrong.

8

THE HANSEN COUNTY MENTAL HEALTH Clinic is a brick building without the first tree. We waited in the waiting room. I was a nervous wreck. Charles tried to act calm.

There was a boy and a man sitting across from us. The man was holding a newspaper in front of his face and the little boy struck a match every minute or two. He'd shake them out and drop them in the trash can.

"Stop striking them matches, Oscar," says the man, not moving his newspaper.

Oscar strikes another match. And in a minute, another one.

"Oscar, I said stop striking the matches."

Oscar strikes another match and the man jerks the paper to his chest and reaches out his hand to hit Oscar's hand but stops short and don't hit him. The match goes out and the man slaps Oscar's hand.

"You retard," says Oscar.

"I'm gonna kill you when we get home."

"I ain't going in there." Then Oscar gets up and starts toward the hall door. His daddy or whoever it was—somehow it didn't feel like his daddy—told him to sit down, but Oscar just stood over by the magazine rack, thumbing through a *National Geographic*.

I felt like I had to say something to help the man out, so I said, "Son, you might burn your house down someday and then you wouldn't have a place to live."

Charles looks at me like I committed the original sin.

"I just told the boy what he needs to be told," I said.

Charles sticks his fingertips up to his temples and slides down into his seat, making the vinyl cover squeak.

About that time a woman comes to the door and asks if we are the Shepherds and then leads us into a nice office with a desk and desk chair, about twenty green plants, and three of those director chairs—orange, green, and yellow. I took the green and Charles took the yellow.

In walks our psychiatric. She introduces herself, Dr. Mary Bridges, sits down and explains all about her background—she got her training in Boston—and about how on Wednesdays she leaves her private practice in Linnville and comes to the clinic to work.

She was tall and wore glasses and had a kind of flat face—almost like a Japanese. She made us feel as comfortable as possible, I suppose. I figured the thing to do was show her that we were normal and just needed some help—that we won't mentally ill in any way.

She went into something about discovering underlying issues and then said, "Let me start by asking if you have any questions."

Lord, I didn't know what to ask *yet*. I felt like I was in a dark room. So in order to relieve a little of the tension I said, "I feel like I'm in the dark." Charles reaches over his shoulder and turns on the light, which we don't need because the sunlight is flooding in through a giant window.

"Charles, that's not what I mean."

Charles turns the light back out.

"Well, you could leave it on," I said.

He turned it back on.

"That'll be fine," says Dr. Bridges. "Let me start by asking how you two met. Charles?"

"Well," says Charles, "I got the library job here at the community college, came up from Atlanta, and had been here several months when I heard Raney singing at the faculty Christmas dinner. I spoke to her afterward and told her how much I enjoyed her singing. I play banjo and was hoping that we might be able to play music together, somehow. Then a few days later she came in the library looking for a Mel Tillis record—"

196

"It won't Mel Tillis," I said.

"Raney, I remember writing it down on the checkout card."

"That must have been some other girl, because—"

"Anyway, whatever it was, we struck up a conversation, and one thing led to another."

"It won't a Mel Tillis record."

"Raney," Dr. Bridges says to me, "let me stick with Charles for a few minutes more, and then you may have a chance to straighten out inconsistencies as you see them. Right now I'm mainly interested in how you and Charles met, and it makes it easier for me to hear from you one at a time."

"Okay," I said. Now I could tell right off that there'd be a lot of mistakes going on here and that I might not get a chance to correct any until it was too late. If Charles spun off a row of six mistakes, not that he'd do that on purpose, by the time he got to number six, I would have lost track. I figured right then and there that I might as well get comfortable with a lot of inaccuracies on the record.

Dr. Bridges was taking notes. "Now," she says, "what do you mean, Charles, 'one thing led to another'?"

"Well, we'd talk in the library about music, mainly. At the time I was collecting some original folk music from the mountains and learning to play banjo. Then we started going out and playing music together."

"What led you to fall in love with and marry Raney?"

"Well, that's hard to say. I mean, you know. She was different from anybody I had ever met— still is. Independent. Very attractive. Beautiful voice. And I think I'd reached a point where I wanted to get married when the right person came along."

"What would you say you liked most about Raney before you were married?"

"Well, I certainly liked the way she looked, although that would be a poor excuse to get married. I liked the way she sang, her honesty and the slightly weird way she looked at things."

"Slightly weird?"

"Well, she would have these stabs of common sense, or something, which would stun me sometimes and I'd never experienced that in a woman before."

"Oh? Okay, well let me—"

"I don't mean that as a sexist statement. What I mean is that I'd never experienced that in anyone I'd dated or anything. On the other hand, I also *assumed,* I guess, that Raney and her family would be able to manage a certain amount of flexibility—that she and her mother and aunts would at least be able to—"

"I'd like to save some of these things until later

198

if I might. Let me give Raney a chance to add any points she might have on your courtship and engagement. Raney, what led you to fall in love with and marry Charles?"

"Listen, my mama and aunts—"

"If at all possible I'd like to save points of disagreement until later—we *will* discuss problem areas in some detail. Let me just ask what led you to fall in love with and marry Charles?"

"Well, one of Charles's strong points was his mind. I've dated better looking boys. And I just liked him a lot and he was easy to talk to and I liked him more and more right up to the day he asked me to marry him and by that time I loved him and had told him so and he'd told me so. Course there was his interest in music and he knew all this background about country music, and Mama and Daddy liked him all right. Or Daddy did. Maybe more than Mama."

"Okay. I just wanted to get an idea of the initial stages of your relationship and your feelings about each other."

"We didn't have a relationship until *after* we got married."

"Excuse me?"

"We didn't have a relationship until *after* we got married—and Charles set that up. I mean I do my part but he sets it up."

"Oh? Oh. No, I don't mean a sexual relationship.

I mean a, ah, regular relationship. Perhaps we can come back to that later."

"Back to what?"

"Your sexual relationship."

"That's not what we're here for."

"Perhaps not, but—Well, let's see, I think at this point I'd like to get some idea of what you feel your problems are. Who'd like to start?"

We just sat there.

"Well," Dr. Bridges says, "perhaps I can say a few more words about what I hope we'll be able to accomplish here." She talked about how conflict could be good and so on for a while, and then asked us what we had in mind to accomplish during our sessions.

Charles spoke right up. "I'd like a third observer," he says. "Someone who is objective. We seem to observe the world from different vantage points. So what we need is—"

"I'm only doing what I think is right," I said. "You think I do what I do because I think what you do is wrong. That's what *you* think. What it is, Dr. Bridges, is Charles's family background and that's not entirely his fault. I don't think—"

"My family background. It doesn't—"

"Wait a minute. You can't—"

"You wait a minute. I was talking first."

"Do you see what I mean, Dr. Bridges? He—"

"Do you see what *I* mean?"

Dr. Bridges says, "Let me see if I can understand what each of you is saying. Charles, you would prefer a third point of view concerning your marriage conflicts. Is that correct?"

"Yes."

"And Raney, you feel that your marriage problems may stem from a difference in early family experiences?"

"I wouldn't say they *stem* from it," I said. "I'd say that's *it*. And it's family background and ways of looking at things. Not just experiences. The main problem is what Charles thinks of my family. My Uncle Nate just, just died, and he blames my mama."

"That is *not* what I said, Raney. You—"

"Just a minute, Charles," says Dr. Bridges. "We'll get back to that. Raney, I don't mean to keep us from talking about problems you're having now. In fact that's probably going to make up a good part of our therapy."

I stared at Dr. Bridges. "What is this therapy part? I didn't know about *that*."

"This is the therapy part," says Dr. Bridges. "Therapy means we work together regularly for a while, talking, trying to understand your marriage in a way that will enable us to solve some of the problems you're having. Okay?"

"Okay," I said.

"Now," she said, "So Raney you believe some of your problems stem from differences in family background?"

"That's right."

"Well," she says, "I think we've identified several starting points. Both of you should know that for some time you may be angry after some of our sessions. We manage to stir up some volatile issues. But over a period of time I'm hoping we'll be able to understand and manage some of those issues. In other words, don't be surprised if you leave a session mad with each other. I'll be seeing you next week, same time if that will work. We'll try to concentrate on the specific misunderstanding you had about your uncle. It would probably be a good idea to work on that only in here and not at home—for a while, anyway."

I guess if we think of all this as going to a *counselor,* it's not so bad. After all, everybody who ever went to school had a counselor. But my counselors never did any counseling like this. All they ever did was come around and explain schedules and give tests and stuff like that. When Sue Blackwell got pregnant and went to Mrs. Darnell, our counselor, Sue ended up having to quit school because of not telling who he was— you know. Everybody but Mrs. Darnell knew it was Paul Gibson.

9

IN OUR SECOND SESSION ABOUT A WEEK AGO we had an awful argument about Uncle Nate. I thought I'd be able to stay calm in front of Dr. Bridges, but some of the things Charles said about Mama and the whole family tore me up. It got me upset so *quick*. It does not make sense—the things he said. I got so mad I couldn't see straight. Finally, we both stopped talking. Then Dr. Bridges talked to us about "point of view," and that made some sense. She had us explain why the other person might say what they did. It was hard to do. She kept wanting us to talk about *feelings*.

Before we left she said it was okay to be mad and that when we got home we might try to write down why we were mad and bring it to the next session, but for us not to *talk* about Uncle Nate for a while, to leave that for the counseling sessions.

Then yesterday in our third session, neither one of us wanted to talk at all and we hadn't written down anything. We just sat there for a minute or so and Dr. Bridges asked if either one of us had a problem to talk about. I had. I had been thinking about Charles's attitude toward my family.

"Well," I said, "I don't want to point fingers

but I think Charles thinks he's too good for my family."

Charles goes right to pieces. "I do not think I'm too good for your family," he says.

"Then why won't you talk to them?"

"I *do* talk to them."

"Oh no you don't. Not like you talk to me. You come home from work and talk to me about what's going on at the library. But have you ever talked to Mama or Daddy about what's going on at the library?"

"Wait a minute," says Charles. "What the hell am I supposed to say to your parents about the library?"

"Charles, you talk to me about the library. Why can't you talk to them about the library? It's nothing but a little simple courtesy."

"Courtesy? I eat with them every single Sunday of my life. What more do you want?"

"Not every single Sunday, Charles. There was that Sunday we—"

"If I may interrupt," says Dr. Bridges. "Raney, how do *you* feel when you and Charles are together with your family?"

"How do *I* feel?"

"Yes."

"Well, I wonder what he's going to say next, if anything, and when he's going to start acting bored."

"How do you feel inside?"

"Well, I don't know. Ready, I guess. Ready for Charles to start acting bored or to upset things."

"Raney, I don't have to—"

"Just a minute, Charles," says Dr. Bridges. "Raney, let me ask Charles a few questions."

Well, she asked Charles a few questions and he hemmed and hawed about feeling uncomfortable and then Dr. Mary Bridges makes this little speech about guess what: family background. I've been trying to talk about it all along but nobody would listen. But then she turns the tables. She says to me:

"Raney, what do you think about Charles's parents? How do you feel about them?"

"Well," I says, "that's different. We don't live in Atlanta. We live in Listre. If we lived in Atlanta I could see coming in here and talking about Charles's parents. But we live in Listre and have a problem right here, so I don't see any need in talking about Charles's parents."

Dr. Bridges explains something about family "patterns" and then you know what she says? She says almost the same thing Aunt Naomi told me one time—that in a sense, families marry families. Wisdom does not reside only in psychiatrics. Aunt Naomi has her share.

"That's what my Aunt Naomi told me one time," I says. "She said a marriage was a marriage of families and not of people and that's why you won't see any whites and coloreds

205

getting married. I'll bet you don't have any married whites and coloreds coming in here do you?"

"No, but I—"

"Well, that's exactly what she said. Said a family marries a family."

I wondered why we were paying to have a psychiatric tell us the very same thing Aunt Naomi could tell us.

"Well, in a certain sense I think you're correct," says Dr. Bridges. "But let me ask you to talk a minute or two about how you feel when you're with Charles's mother and father."

"Well, I don't see them that much, but when I do, they seem a little bit uppity or something— know it all, and they won't spend much time sitting down, just with me, and talking about something I know about. They glance around off all kinds of topics I'm not interested in, like the politics in Atlanta and such. I don't feel any connection to them, even like I feel to my own kin folks I don't hardly know.

"Charles's mama and daddy are on a different level from me and you can tell by the way they act that they think it's a *higher* level. Of course the last word's not in on that. And they put all this emphasis on correct English—which I don't always use. I mean they talk *about* it. They keep saying the language is dying—which I don't understand. How could the language be dying when all these people I know are talking the same way they always did? I think Charles's mama and daddy just maybe ought to pay more attention to who they talk to. *What* somebody ends up talking about seems to me has a lot to do with how much your language is dying. And talking about language dying seems to me to be a dead subject to talk about.

"And they're always talking about some book they just read which I hadn't ever heard of. They were talking about a best seller before the wedding and I merely said the Bible was the best seller every year and it had never once been beat and they looked at me like I was crazy. That kind of thing."

"I'm sorry, our time is about up," says Dr. Bridges. "We'll certainly follow up on this, Raney, and perhaps gain insight into some of your problems by looking at both of your family backgrounds. I'd like for each of you to think about the marriages in your family—parents, aunts, uncles, and so forth. Think about their problems, relationships, marital habits, and we'll discuss that and see what we come up with."

So I got to thinking. The first thing I came up with is: there are not any men in our whole family—those that are close to us—except Daddy. And he sort of sits back and watches things go by. So it's hard for me to think about marriages when all the men have died.

We started talking about it on the way home and talked and talked and talked. Some of the ways our marriage is going is like other marriages in our families—almost like our marriages are kin. Rules get set by somebody hundreds of years ago and they are hard to break, like rules about what you can and can't talk about.

It finally came up. In our session yesterday, the fourth one, Dr. Bridges asked us about our "sexual relationship."

Neither one of us spoke. I looked at my hands in my lap and Charles bent over and scratched his ankle through his sock.

"Do you both feel comfortable with your sexual relationship?"

"I didn't know we'd have to talk about that," I said.

"Well, no topic is off limits; although we may decide that this or some other topic is not really necessary."

"I certainly think our sexual relationship is okay," I said. "I don't think we need to talk about it in here."

"What about you, Charles?"

Charles didn't speak for a few seconds. Then his eyebrows went up and the corners of his mouth went down. "Well, I don't know."

"Oh Lord, Charles," I says, "you're not going to get into *that*." I looked at Dr. Bridges. "I just think there are some things we ought not to talk about. Some things are natural, and best left alone."

"Listen, Raney," says Charles, "you speak for yourself. You think—"

"I am speaking for myself. You think that just because—"

"Let me speak for myself, Raney," says Charles. "You say you don't want to talk about it. Fine. That doesn't mean—"

"Charles, if you're going to get into that filthy stuff, I'm going to leave. That's all there is to it."

Dr. Bridges interrupts. "Raney, I'd like to have a short discussion with Charles pertaining to your sexual relationship. I—"

"He can talk about his relationship but not mine."

"Raney," says Charles, "You can't separate—"

"Just a minute, Charles," says Dr. Bridges. "Raney, I would like to talk briefly with Charles about his feelings about your sexual relationship. I can understand if you're uncomfortable with that and we can make other arrangements."

"What kind of other arrangements?"

"Well, we can arrange separate sessions for a while, or one together and then one separate and so on."

"No, that's okay. Go ahead." I couldn't imagine Charles in there alone with her—talking about *us*.

"I'll tell you what," says Dr. Bridges, "if you

find you have a strong reaction to something Charles says just write it down on this pad with this pen and when we finish, you and I can discuss any reaction you might have had—if you like. How does that sound?"

"Okay, but I didn't know we were going to come in here and tell secrets."

"I hope that'll not exactly be the case. Let's try it this way and see how it works. If you would, Raney, move your chair sort of back there so your writing won't distract Charles."

I moved my chair.

"Okay, Charles, where would you like to start?" says Dr. Bridges.

"About what?" says Charles.

"Well, about how you feel about your sexual relationship with Raney."

(So I wrote: *I didn't know we were going to come in here and tell secrets. Some things should be left alone.*)

"Well, I feel it's okay, generally. I do feel we should be able to discuss it more. I have felt rather confined in what few discussions we've had, as well as in the carrying out of the actual, ah, act itself. Raney is very reluctant to talk about the whole subject of sex." (I was getting worried. I wrote again: *He'd better not say anything about our honeymoon.*) "I believe if we could talk about sex then that could get things going," says Charles. *(Get things going! He's told me over and over how wonderful I am—warm, and everything. Whispers to me. And now this. He's never talked to me about getting things going. I can't believe this.)*

"Specifically, what would you like to talk about with Raney?"

"Well, Raney isn't interested in doing some of the . . . some of the, ah, things, I'd like for her, or for us, to do." *(He's going to say it. I know he is. Our honeymoon is our private business. This is getting out of hand.)*

"Let me see if I hear you correctly," says Dr. Bridges. "You basically have some problems about your and Raney's predisposition to discuss sex. And you believe that open discussions could perhaps alleviate some of the problems you experience while or before actually making love. Is that accurate?"

"Essentially, yes."

"Then let me stop for a minute. Raney, I notice you've been writing."

"I sure have. I think this is getting out of hand."

"I can assure you that I will pass no judgment on anything that is discussed here. I do believe if we discuss problems openly we can begin to recognize basic feelings, and that that can perhaps help all three of us understand some of what's going on—with some clarity."

"I don't think there's anything to discuss. I don't want to discuss sex and filth."

Charles breaks in: "Raney, you don't have to—"

"Just a minute, Charles," says Dr. Bridges. "Raney, I would be glad to discuss what you perceive as filth—if you'd like to talk about that for a minute."

"He thinks he can read filthy magazines and then take me out on my one and only honeymoon and read filthy sections out of his head that come from the very pages of that magazine—all this in our own honeymoon room—when I never had the slightest idea any boy I would ever date, much less marry, could ever have such ideas. And then—"

"Raney, you can't say that I was—"

"Just a minute, Charles," says Dr. Bridges. "Raney, let me assure you that it's all right to talk about this."

"No, you all go ahead and talk, if that's what's got to be done. I'll write. I've done said too much."

(So I wrote some more: *I think you can get some things out in the clear and that's the best thing in the world to do. But not necessarily— like when Harold Sikes's German shepherd threw up Fred Woolard's pet rabbit at the church barbecue that time.*)

Dr. Bridges ended the session. "Let's try to pick up here next time. I'd like to suggest that we leave our present discussion here in the room if possible, rather than take it with you. The subject, as you see, creates a good bit of tension. Raney, would you like for me to read what you've written or would you like to keep it, and perhaps bring it back next time?"

"You can have it," I said. I handed it to her.

We walked to the car without speaking.

I was so mad at Charles I didn't know what to do. I was in a rage. I decided not to speak until at least after we passed the Triple A Rent-All. Charles didn't speak either, so about a mile past the Triple A, I said: "Charles, I think you got a lot of gall going into that psychiatric's office and—"

"Raney, she's a psychologist. A psychologist! Can you say psychologist? Psy-cho-lo-gist?"

"Yes, but that has absolutely nothing to do with it and you know it. You're trying to change the subject so you—"

"Just say it, Raney! Let me hear you *say* the *word*."

"Charles, if you're going to start hollering you can stop the car and let me out. I'll just walk home. It's bad enough already, without that. You had a lot of nerve going into a psychiatric's office and—"

"Jesus H. Christ, Raney!"

"Okay, stop the car. STOP THE CAR."

"Raney, I'm not going to stop the—"

"STOP THE DAMN CAR."

I've never been so upset in all my life. Here I

213

was, cussing right there in the front seat of our Dodge Dart. I felt humiliated.

Charles wouldn't stop the car. He wouldn't even speak. He kept driving—his knuckles white on the steering wheel, his chin stuck out so far it about touched the windshield.

I didn't speak again until we passed the Tastee Freeze. I figured I'd wait until we got to the Tastee Freeze to see if Charles would speak.

"You got a lot of nerve," I said, "going in there and telling a stranger all those things."

"Raney, I didn't tell her anything. If you want to stop going to the marriage counselor—fine. Otherwise, that's what therapy is about: talking. Talking about problems."

"Anybody can talk about problems. Howdy Doody can talk about problems. Charles, if you ever tell her what you said to me on our honeymoon I'll never speak to you again as long as I live."

I'll tell you, I do not understand men. Charles figures the minute we're married he can start acting like a African Brahma bull. There I was on my honeymoon night, a virgin—well, almost— laying in bed, and my husband standing in front of the Mary Tyler Moore Show with nothing on but his Fruit of the Loom, drinking champagne out of a plastic cup, looking at me with a grin that would have moved mountains. And then he started talking. I will not repeat the things he said but I will say they were unnatural. And I did not hesitate saying so that very night: "Charles, that is disgusting," I said. "That is something niggers would do." (He always perks up when I say nigger, but that time didn't even phrase him.)

"Raney, honey." He kept calling me honey. "It's okay. Try it. Try it."

"You never seen dogs do that, Charles. Don't you see," I said, "dogs wouldn't even do that."

Let me tell you the truth. I can see a man bringing up something like that after he's been married for a year or two. I can even understand Charles picking this up in a book somewhere. I won't born yesterday. But what got to me was him standing there in the middle of that floor talking that way before our marriage was ever consumed, or whatever it is—before we ever did the act of love intended for a husband and wife on their first night of marriage.

I've read *The Flame and the Flower.* I know a little something about pornography. But what could I do? One of the most important parts of the honeymoon was ruined as far as I was concerned: the very reason for a honeymoon. Charles had blew the whole thing.

I don't know what's going to happen in these marriage counseling sessions. It seemed like they were good and now I don't know. We do need a little something to get us straightened out like

Aunt Flossie said, but I never had any idea we'd be plowing down into things which are nobody's business. I've forgiven Charles for the way he behaved on our honeymoon. And I've told him so. We all make mistakes. I've made my share. But I don't understand what good it can do to dig up all this sex stuff.

One of the good things me and Charles have finally agreed on is to try to listen to each other. From the time we first get in a argument neither one of us usually ever pays any attention to what the other one is saying. I know it's true. So we've agreed that when we have an argument only one person will talk for a while and the other person will listen. *Then,* the person listening will have to explain how the other person *feels* about what's going on. We actually went through this procedure during our last session when we had a argument about . . . well, I can't remember what it was about. I think it's a good idea. But it's hard.

Now if we *do* talk about sex in a counseling session, I won't know what to say. Charles is the one who sets things up, as I said. He figures out the time and place and we just do it. Usually in bed where it's supposed to be done of course. There was that one time on the rug. That was certainly different. And it did make me feel kind of brazen or whatever the word is. I guess if Charles and me did talk about it, I could say that

216

I didn't mind that on the rug and it would be all right with me if we did it in there again. I kind of liked the way the rug felt on my back.

Oh well, maybe I can suggest it sometime. That's what all these E.R.A. people are starting to say: that women can do about whatever they want to. *Cosmopolitan.* My Lord. But I would feel very unnatural taking over the man's position like they talk about. I just couldn't do it.

PART THREE
The Feed Room

1

DR. BRIDGES AGREED FOR US TO STOP therapy after seven sessions and see how things go for a while. We don't stay mad so long at a time as we did and we're able to say how we feel better than we were before.

I've got a new part time job.

Daddy's store—the Hope Road General Store—is at the intersection of Crossville and Hope Roads. It's a normal general store with a porch on the front and a feed room built onto the side and three gas pumps out front. Daddy's had it as long as I can remember. When I was little I used to go with him out there some nights and help. I'd wait on a few people while he watched and he'd let me make price signs with crayons and meat wrapping paper. And I would go into the feed room where the feed sacks were as big as me and tight as ticks and smelled musky and I'd climb up on them and crawl around until Daddy came in and got me and we started home.

I stopped in yesterday morning when I was coming back from the dentist. I walked in and stood just inside the door.

In the back, behind the stove, was Uncle Nate's wicker bottom chair—with the little flat navy blue pillow. It hit me all of a sudden that I could take Uncle Nate's place—in a way. I had been thinking about doing some part time work. Daddy gives Charles and me money—he insists. I hate to *keep* taking it, but he won't talk about it, or else goes on and on about how he don't want us to have the same hard times that him and Mama had when they started out.

The store definitely needs a woman. First of all, right in the middle of the bread section—which is just inside the door—is this great big minnow tank which they don't keep cleaned out good. The water's so muddy you could drive a fence post down in it. And it smells. Who's going to want to buy a loaf of bread standing there beside that mudhole with several dead suffocated minnows floating on top?

The thing to do is clean that thing up and move it to the back where the overalls and water buckets and wash tubs and stuff like that is. Then we could put a sign up in the bread section saying MINNOW TANK IN BACK.

Sneeds Perry, who as I said is running the place, will sit with a toothpick in his mouth watching the air move while the floor fills up with cigarette butts and the bottle cap holder on the drink box gets so full that your bottle cap just plings down onto the floor and rolls up under something.

But Sneeds is generally nice. That's why I think I could work with him. And Daddy said the other day that it was going to be hard to find part

222

time help to take Uncle Nate's place. I could take care of the stuff inside while Sneeds pumps gas. Like I say, this all hit me out of the clear blue. It seemed like just the thing to do.

Sneeds was working on a radio that was sitting on a shelf over behind the cash register. He had the front off and was doing something to it with a screw driver.

I spoke to him. He looked over his shoulder and said, "Howdy, Raney." Then I walked along the canned and boxed food aisles. Some of the food had just about disappeared under dust: there were cans of corn that could *grow* corn.

Then there are all those shelves built into the front windows. They're so stuffed you can't see out. Or in. There are hats and boots and oil cans all stuck in there. And combs and handkerchiefs on these dusty cardboard displays. I figured I could have all that cleaned out and Windexed in a afternoon. Just that little bit of work would change the whole atmosphere.

I knew I'd be a real asset to the place and if Sneeds and Daddy and Charles all said okay, I'd be in.

I walked over to the cash register and said, "Sneeds, you need a woman's touch around this place."

"That's for sure," he says. He put down his screw driver, turned around and shifted his toothpick. "What you got in mind?" Sneeds always wears a little black toboggin, engineer boots, rolled up dungarees, and a flannel shirt—summer or winter.

"Well, if I worked in here part time for a while I could have this place looking real nice. What I mean is I got some ideas about moving things around, you know: rearranging a bit. To help sales go up. Then too, when you have to go out and pump gas I could stay in here and watch things."

"Fine with me," he says. "I'll tell you there's plenty of woman's work around here and like I always said: a woman's work is for a woman. I hate it. Talk to your Daddy."

I'll say he hates it. "Then it'd be all right with you?"

"Sure."

That was easy enough. So I drove to Mama's and Daddy's. Daddy's truck was out front. He was in the kitchen drinking a cup of coffee and eating a piece of pound cake like he's done just about every day of his life.

"Afternoon," he says. "Where you been?"

"I've been to the dentist. Fourteen dollars—just for a cleaning. Listen Daddy, I've got a idea: why don't I start working at the store?"

"What's the matter with you, honey? You don't need a job."

"Daddy, it would just be part time. That store is a mess. And with Uncle Nate gone now—you need somebody part time. If I move a few things around in there and get it cleaned up, you'll do a better business. I guarantee it."

"Honey, don't nothing much but farmers come in there. We sell more cigarettes, drinks, chicken wire, fence posts, and such than anything else. No need to try to make it into something that won't have no market."

"I don't mean change it. I mean make it better. That fish tank stuck in the bread section is just awful. It ought to be moved to the back. The place needs a woman's touch. All I want to do is go in there a few afternoons a week after I get the housework done. It'd give me a chance to talk to people and make a little spending money." Daddy didn't say anything. "Don't you think it'd be all right, Mama?"

"Well, I don't know. Maybe. Until you all start thinking about raising a family." She was drying the last dinner dish.

"Now, honey," said Daddy, "I told you not to worry about money for a while. You know I don't want you going through the troubles me and your mama had."

"Daddy, I'm getting bored at home. I need a place to work—part time at least."

Daddy stuck the last piece of cake in his mouth and put down his fork. "I'm not so sure it'll be as much fun as you think it will," he said with his mouth full of cake, losing a couple of crumbs;

225

"but if you've got your mind set on it, go ahead. I'll tell you what, try it for one week and then let me know what you think."

I hugged his neck and told him to brush the crumbs off his chin.

Next, Charles.

It was Friday, so Charles had cooked: pork chops, new potatoes, and some early turnip salet Aunt Flossie had brought by. He's been cooking on Friday nights because he says it helps him unwind from the library.

"Charles, this pork chop is delicious," I said. "I declare, we're going to have to open you up a restaurant."

"Thanks."

"Listen, Charles, not to change the subject, but I want to work at Daddy's store. Full time." (I figured I'd give myself room to compromise down to three-fourths and finally to half time.)

"Raney, we don't need the money. Your father said he'd help us get on our feet. You know he wouldn't want you working at that store."

"He said it would be fine. I asked him this afternoon."

Charles sat there looking at me and chewing on a piece of pork chop long after it was chewed up. "Your daddy said okay?"

"He sure did. You're so cute."

"Raney, you'd get tired of it. Why do you want to work at that store?"

"It needs a woman's touch. And it'd be fun. I stopped in there this afternoon and that's exactly what it needs—a woman's touch. That place could be fixed up real nice, so housewives would enjoy shopping in there. That minnow tank had two dead minnows in it and there's Sneeds Perry working on a radio; and most of the time he's sitting out by the front door, leaning up against the side of the building with a toothpick in his mouth, counting to see which is most that day: Fords or Chevrolets."

"Raney, you can't just walk in there and change that place around. And you know what kind of people go in there all the time."

"No, I don't," I said. "What kind of people go in there all the time?"

"Well, housewives don't—much. They go to the Piggly Wiggly in Bethel."

"What kind of people do go in there then?"

"A bunch of men who . . . who stand around and spit on the floor."

"Charles, there are three oil cans with dirt in the bottom over by the stove for people to spit in."

"It's not the clientele you should be around all day."

"Please tell me what that is supposed to mean."

"What it means is: the people who hang around that store are a bunch of rednecks—in the truest sense."

"Charles, Uncle Nate used to work out there, and my own flesh and blood daddy happens to own it, and he 'hangs around' out there."

"Look, Raney, it would never work. It would never work. I just don't want you stuck in that store all day. Especially with Sneeds Perry."

"Charles Shepherd, you've got to be kidding. Sneeds is as harmless as a flea. The main reason Daddy has him there is Sneeds knows everybody and has a real easy way about him with the customers. It's his cousin Sam that causes all the problems. And he's honest. That's what I've heard Daddy say. And for heaven's sake, he's got rotten teeth and wears the same clothes all the time." (The thing is, I've never actually *smelled* Sneeds. Daddy says he has just three shirts and that he'll wear them for two or three days each and then he'll wear this sweater one day—the day he's getting the shirts cleaned. Then he starts over again. But he's never actually smelled as far as I could ever tell.) "I'll tell you what, Charles: if you're so worried, I'll work just three-fourths time."

"Raney, we don't need the money."

"I'm getting bored staying home and I don't feel right about keeping on taking handouts from Daddy, Charles."

Charles chews for a while. "Your Daddy wouldn't be happy unless he was helping us out."

"Maybe so, but that's off the subject. . . ."

"Raney, I don't think—"

"Okay, okay, okay. Half time—but then I might as well not be working at all. Half time; I'll do it half time."

Charles chewed some more. "Go ahead. I don't want to be the one to stop you. But don't say I didn't warn you."

"Warn me about what?"

"You won't like it."

"I bet I will."

While Charles cleaned up after supper, he left the strainer out of the sink and the water turned on, but I was so happy about him saying yes about me working, I didn't say anything about it. But I do need to mention it next time. In marriage counseling we talked about how you shouldn't carry around little grudges because they grow bigger and uglier while you carry them around. Next time he leaves the strainer out, I'll mention it.

2

THE SUBJECT OF ME WORKING CAME UP AT Sunday dinner at Mama's just before I went to work on Monday. Aunt Naomi, Aunt Flossie, Norris, and Mary Faye were there, and so was Preacher Gordon. Mama invites him about twice a year. I like him a lot but Charles seems a little less certain.

Preacher Gordon asked the blessing of course—a right long one—and we started passing the food around. While he helped his plate, Preacher Gordon talked about the family that had come down during the invitation that morning. They transferred their letter and rededicated their lives to Christ—except for their teenage son. His hair was about dragging the floor. They were from Maryland, I think. Moved here to work at the new G.E. plant. Charles has been going to church more regular lately and was there that morning. The secret is not to ask him to go. He's also been talking to Mr. Ford and Mr. Clawson after the service about fishing in their ponds. I told him if they said okay to be sure to ask them to go with him when he went. You can tell they like the attention Charles gives them about fishing.

Aunt Naomi, while she's passing the cornbread, says, "What's this I hear about you working at the store, Raney?"

I wondered, from the tone of her voice, what she was getting at. "That's right," I said. "Part time, for a while anyway. I was getting bored at home and that store needs a woman's touch, inside at least."

"I been bored at home plenty times myself," says Aunt Naomi. "But you know, when you think about it, there's more than enough to do around a house—if it's done right I mean—to keep a body busy."

"It sure is," I said. "But Charles helps me."

"Well, you know, I mean stuff a woman needs to do." Aunt Naomi was salting her mashed potatoes.

Norris took Mary Faye's biscuit. She grabbed at it and Mama made him give it back.

"I think a man can do anything a woman can do in the home," said Charles. "As long as the woman will turn loose and let him." Charles looked at me and squinted his eyes.

"That's fine and good," says Aunt Naomi. "I agree there is a *place* for a husband in the home—helping out some, but. . . ." She looked around and settled on Preacher Gordon. "I mean some of this getting out of our places is what you preached about that Sunday, Preacher Gordon— Charles, I don't think you were there—about all that's going on out in society these days."

"Well," Preacher Gordon said. He laughed. "That's right, but Raney said 'part time.' She's probably not considering leaving the home full time, especially if she and Charles decide to have some little ones."

"I have a question for you about that," says Charles.

"Sure," says Preacher Gordon.

Mama says, "Now I want us to enjoy our dinner. Maybe we ought to talk about something else."

There was a pause.

"These biscuits are delicious, Doris," said Preacher Gordon. "And everything else. MMMummm."

"He's just going to ask a question," says Aunt Flossie.

"I think it's all right to talk about it," I said.

"I just hate to talk about politics at the dinner table," says Mama.

"This ain't politics, Mama," I said.

"Well, whatever."

"What's your question?" asks Aunt Flossie.

"I was wondering," says Charles to Preacher Gordon, "suppose Raney and I had a full time job each, *and* a baby. Not that we will, but suppose. I'm just wondering how you relate that set-up to the scriptures, Mr. Gordon? Or do you?"

"Well, I'll be happy to talk about that," said Preacher Gordon. "And to also give some indication of how—"

"You didn't get the pickle dish, did you?" says Aunt Naomi, handing the pickle dish to Preacher Gordon. She was across from him.

"Yes, I did. I don't care for any—well, maybe I'll take one of these."

"They're the sweet. Do you like the sweet?"

"Oh, yes. And to, ah, give some indication, Charles, of *how* I go about answering a question like that for myself."

"Dill is my favorite," says Aunt Naomi.

I hadn't thought about Charles and me both

working and having a baby all at the same time, but if something happened to Daddy. . . . Charles does not make a very big salary at the college. So I was interested in what Preacher Gordon had to say. I had missed that sermon too, I think. It must have been the Sunday we left after Sunday School to go to Williamsburg. Charles had insisted we leave after Sunday School.

"First I go to the Bible," says Preacher Gordon. "I have to either find a direct answer itself or a firm foundation for an answer which I would hope I could find in the life of Jesus. It's surprising how much territory the parables and the Sermon on the Mount cover. Then, of course, there are the letters of Paul and so forth."

"So how would you relate this hypothetical case I just mentioned to the scriptures?" asks Charles.

"Doris, did you put lemon in the tea?" says Aunt Naomi.

"Naomi, let him finish," said Aunt Flossie.

"Yes, I did," said Mama. "Did you want lemon in your tea, Preacher Gordon?"

"Oh, yes. I've got some, I believe."

"I just couldn't see any," says Aunt Naomi. "Oh, there it is, under your ice. Oh my, there's mine too! Doris, you must have put the lemon in first, *then* the ice."

"That's the way I always do it," said Mama. "That way it gets mixed in with—"

"Wait a minute!" I practically shouted. "I want to hear this about working. I never thought about it being in the Bible."

"Simply put," said Preacher Gordon, and wiped his mouth, "I believe the scripture is quite clear on this. The man is the head of the household, the breadwinner so to speak, and the woman is the natural mother of course, whose principal responsibility is to the home itself: especially the raising up of the children under God's word and laws. And then too we understand, or I understand, from the Old Testament that Adam was made by God, in the image of God, *for* God, and that Eve was made by God, from the man, *for* the man."

"Well, that's a clear answer," says Charles. "I mean—let me ask you this first: if it's clear in the scriptures, you don't have to think about it very much, do you? I mean if it's there, it's there."

"Well, yes. But I can only speak for myself."

"My problem," says Charles, "is that it's not all that clear to me." Charles seemed very calm. "So I've had to think about it and of course that's okay: to think about it. Right?"

I didn't know Charles had been thinking about all that. I imagine Charles thinks about several things at once sometimes.

"Certainly it's okay to think about it. That's why God gave us a mind: to use. No problem there."

"The way I see it," says Charles, "Jesus said, 'Do unto others as you would have them do unto you.' That means I have to help Raney out at home because I would have her help me out if we switched positions. But if we both worked, we'd both do the same amount of work at home. It seems only fair that way, or just. And justice is what God is all about. *I* think. That's a little more general than your interpretation."

"You know," said Aunt Naomi, "on that 'do unto others as you'd have them do unto you,' you *could* say that you ought to give somebody all your money because that's what you'd want them to do to you, but then if everybody did that, there'd be nobody to *take* any money because you wouldn't want somebody to take yours, and if the Devil could talk somebody into it, that somebody would go around taking all the money and end up the richest person in the world while everybody else was poor. We talked about that in Sunday School one time."

"That's not exactly what I'm talking about, somehow," said Charles. "See, Mr. Gordon, I think societal expectations play a large part in all this. For example, society sees men as fulfilling about one thousand jobs, and women—about three or four: housewives, secretaries, teachers, and nurses. That doesn't seem exactly fair to me—or just. It seems to me that if societal expectations are unjust then the church ought to be doing, or at least saying, something about that."

"In some ways I agree about society expectations," said Preacher Gordon. "But I worry about government expectations, too. You know, the whims of society and government shift like the sands. What's in today is out tomorrow. We need to—"

"Build our houses on a *rock*," says Aunt Naomi.

"God's truth has been God's truth for so long," says Mama, pointing with her fork, "and I know the joy I've felt in raising my children is a joy from God and I thank God for people like you, Preacher Gordon, who have been called to interpret the Gospel."

"I guess the whole point I wanted to make," says Charles, "is that it's not all so simple and clear to me about a man's role and a woman's role. Surely the social customs of biblical times influenced the scriptures. Wouldn't you say, Preacher Gordon?"

"Perhaps," said Preacher Gordon, "but then again, divine inspiration has a certain time-lessness about it."

"I mean slavery didn't seem to be a burning issue back then," says Charles.

I didn't want to get into all that.

"That's why tinkering with the scriptures bothers me so much," said Mama. "All those translations. I read somewhere they had computers working on one of those new translations. That takes the cake." She got up and brought the tea jug.

I could see what Charles was talking about. I'd never thought about it before.

"I'll tell you what I don't like," says Aunt Naomi, "is the idea of all this government day care stuff. That's pretty much like the communists, ain't it, Preacher Gordon? Seems like we're getting more like them and they're getting more like us. They're wearing dungarees all over the place. Pretty soon we'll be all the same. That's what I'm afraid of. I heard not long ago that *England* is going communist."

"You mean 'socialist,' " says Charles. "Except they've been that way a long time."

"That was it: socialist," says Aunt Naomi. "That's what I heard—that they're going socialist. And did you know that they have day care centers on just about every street corner in Russia?"

"Aunt Naomi," I said. "What if all the communists started wearing green shirts. It'd be all right for me to wear one, wouldn't it?"

"Well, yes, but . . . if we happened to have a war and somebody started shooting all the communists, you might get shot. You wouldn't want to wear a green shirt *then.* That's another thing: the way women are dressing like men. It's unnatural."

"How about some more cabbage, Preacher Gordon?" I said.

"Oh, no thanks. Well, maybe just a little. It's all mighty good, Doris."

We all said it sure was.

The communists didn't have a thing to do with it.

"What do you think about me working and having a baby, Daddy?" I asked.

"Jimmy Pope called me a communist," said Norris.

"Be quiet," said Mary Faye.

"Well," said Daddy, "we'll have to see about all that when the time comes. You ain't pregnant, are you?"

"Oh no."

So we didn't talk about it any more. We drifted off to talking about the Blue Ridge Parkway.

Preacher Gordon ate a lot. He's not bashful about that. Mama says that's one thing she likes about him. And he shook Charles's hand when we left and said he'd like to talk to Charles some more. I think Charles likes him better now that he's got to know him over a meal and found out he is not iron clad like Mr. Brooks—who threatened to stop singing in the choir because Mr. Phillips, the choir director, was against the church buying a bus. Of all things.

"Charles," I said, while we were driving home, "I wish you felt like staying a little longer on

Sunday afternoons. All we're doing is sitting and talking. It really don't hurt, does it?"

"As a matter of fact, it does hurt. I can't just sit in one place like that for a whole afternoon and talk about, about God knows what all, or who all. I do think I like talking to Mr. Gordon, better than I thought I would, better than I like his sermons. Maybe I can start talking to him about his sermons. I'll bet nobody else in that church does. I mean really talking."

"I'm talking about Mama and them, mainly. I'd like to visit more—sometimes other than just on Sundays, but—"

"Go. Visit during the week."

"Charles, you know it wouldn't seem right—me traipsing in to see Aunt Naomi once a week with you sitting at home with your nose in a book and Aunt Naomi asks, 'Where's Charles?' and I say, 'Sitting at home with his nose in a book.'"

"That would be okay with me."

"I know it would, because it's not *your* reputation."

"Reputation?"

"Charles, the entire foundation of my entire family is built on visiting. The family that visits together stays together. And if—"

"What if they didn't stay together, Raney? What would happen then?"

"Wait a minute. I haven't finished. And how do you think I feel walking into a room full of my aunts, uncles, and cousins when the living husband that I'm married to is at home reading Robinson Crusoe or something. It's like walking in beside a blank spot, or one of them black holes, Charles. Now I could—"

"Raney, there are plenty of singles at your family gatherings."

"I haven't finished. Oh no, they aren't 'singles.' Uncle Frank is dead, Uncle Forrest is dead, and now Uncle Newton. My widow aunts don't count as singles. And their husbands didn't ever sit at home reading."

"Maybe that's why they're all dead."

"Charles. Charles, that's simply awful."

"Okay, I'm sorry."

"What I was going to say is: you wouldn't have to come every single, solitary time. The way it is now, if I visited regularly by myself they'd all forget who I was married to."

"Wear a name tag saying, 'My husband is Charles—male, 5' 10", loves to read—especially today.' I'll get one made up—I swear."

"I don't think it's funny. I think it's important."

3

SNEEDS AND ME GOT ALONG FINE THE FIRST week at the store. Monday—the day I started— he let me do the candy order. I had to check the items on the order sheet. The salesman says,

"Two boxes Baby Ruth, two Butterfingers, one Powerhouse." He was going so fast I had to keep stopping him. Sneeds said that was the thing to do. He said a delivery man gypped him out of some potato chips one time and some magazines another time.

The part I like best about working in the store is finding something for somebody when I know where it is and they don't. Somebody will come in, look around for a minute, then come over and say, "Do you have any Kleenex?" And I say "Sure do," and come around from behind the counter and go straight to it. It's like being in a spelling bee and getting the easiest word.

Right off the bat—that first day—I told Sneeds that the minnow tank had to be moved.

He says, "Do you know how much that thing weighs?"

"No, but if you'd scoop out all the dead minnows and mud it'd probably be down to about twenty pounds and you could slide it wherever you wanted to."

He laughed. He's got rotten teeth and he's about thirty-five or forty I think, and he moves real slow. But he keeps the books and Daddy says he's accurate and he just hopes he can keep him.

"Well," says Sneeds, "besides the fact that that tank weighs about a thousand pounds, you've got the problem of that big wall socket for the filter and light and all that. There ain't another one anywhere except on that post right there beside the tank. You'd have to put in another wall socket."

"I'll talk to Daddy about that," I said.

Also on that first day I found a feather duster under the counter. But you will not believe what else I found under there. There were these boxes of preventatives. There were all kinds of makes and models. It embarrassed me to death.

Well, that's okay. People have to get them somewhere.

I tried to dust off the canned food with the feather duster but what I needed was a vacuum cleaner. All the feather duster did was move the dirt somewhere else. So Thursday morning I brought my Kirby and by lunch I had the canned and boxed food cleaned up and by Friday I had the windows squeaky clean and all the junk cleaned off those shelves. Even Sneeds was pleased. The whole place looked like you'd opened window shades on a sunny morning. I moved out those oil cans from around the stove and got three brass-colored spittoons from Pope's, cleaned the ceilings, the bathroom, the shelves, and throwed out nine big garbage bags of pure-t trash.

The only problem was that even before I finished, one of Sneeds's buddies, Lennie somebody, came in and said, "Hell, I might as well be in the g. d. Seven-Eleven, Sneeds!"

Monday, when I put the feather duster back under the counter I noticed these stacks of magazines under there. Girlie magazines. *Playboy*, *Penthouse*, and some other one. In my daddy's own store. I could not believe it. My mind shot ahead six or seven years and I saw a little boy or girl of mine rustling under that counter and seeing a picture of a unnatural act which would stick in their mind forever as the way it's supposed to be. In my daddy's own store.

"Sneeds, why do you have those magazines stuck under the counter?" I said. "Why don't you put them out on the rack with all the others?"

"They ain't your regular magazines," says Sneeds. "We might get a little trouble from some of the church people."

I've already heard two or three men around the store talking about "the people down at the church."

"Well," I said, "how does anybody know about those magazines if they're stuck behind the counter?"

"Oh, they know. They know. There's regular customers who come in here as soon as we get in a new shipment."

'Well, don't expect me to sell any."

"Okay, I won't. Just holler for me."

That beat all. Here this had been going on under the whole community's nose for no telling how long. In my daddy's own general store. I figured I'd just have to say something to Daddy about it.

I finally had a chance after Sunday dinner when he went back to the bedroom to take his usual Sunday nap; I followed him.

"Daddy, I know about them magazines under the counter at the store."

"Honey, now you leave those magazines alone."

"Daddy, that's not what I'm talking about. How can you go to church and still sell those magazines? I can't do it. Everytime somebody wants one I call Sneeds. Why do you sell them?"

"Honey, Sneeds manages all of that. I give him free rein in ordering and the whole magazine idea is his. I asked him about those magazines myself and he said their profit margin is higher than anything in the store. If you want to talk to Sneeds about stopping the magazines—fine. I just hate to put a man in control of something and then pull the rug out from under him. Plus, they're out of sight. He keeps them out of sight."

"I just think it's wrong, Daddy."

"Well, let me think about it. That's all I know to say now. I hate to let Sneeds do something and then tell him not to do it."

So I decided I would try to talk to Sneeds again. Monday afternoon—of the second week—during a lull, I'm sweeping inside and Sneeds is sitting out front in the sunshine. I go out and stand in front of him, putting the shadow of my head across his eyes.

"Sneeds, don't you think those magazines under the counter are filthy?"

"They ain't filthy—necessarily," he says. "They don't hurt nobody as far as I can tell. These people'll buy them somewheres. We might as well make the money as somebody else."

"Well, I just don't think it's right. If it was, they wouldn't have to be under the counter. You know the expression 'under the counter'?"

"Well, yes, but if you put them out where everybody can see them, old Mr. Brooks is liable to have the sheriff on us."

"Well, I just think it's wrong to sell them at all and I wish you'd think about stopping."

"Do you know how much money they bring in?"

"No."

"A lot. One heck of a lot."

There didn't seem to be much I could do. I put out some tracts—"What the Bible Means to Me"—but they didn't go very fast. The magazines sold steady. (I must admit that I couldn't help laughing at some of the cartoons in *Playboy*. That's all I looked at though—for any length of time. The pictures of the naked women are hazy like they're in a dream. And I cannot believe they show *everything* like they do—so the men can go off somewhere and look at the pictures. I mean you don't ever see some man sitting on the front porch or out in the yard looking at *Playboy*, do you? No. They're too embarrassed.)

Madora told me about *Playgirl*, but I don't care to see one. I wonder if they have the men all hazy like in a dream like in *Playboy*. I think it would be better if they had them sweaty—kind of shiny, maybe like they just got off working in the fields on a hot day. But I haven't seen one and I don't plan to.

For two days I'd noticed this brand new broom— with a piece of thin cardboard around the thistles—sitting by the cash register, but I hadn't thought anything about it until Mrs. Johnson, who had just bought three bags of groceries, took a look at her receipt after Sneeds had torn it off the cash register.

"What's this here?" she said, pointing to the receipt.

"Oh. That's the broom," says Sneeds.

"I didn't get no broom," says Mrs. Johnson.

"That there ain't your broom?" says Sneeds.

"Oh, no. I didn't get no broom."

"I declare, I'm awful sorry, Mrs. Johnson. Let me put this back where it belongs. I imagine somebody must have left it standing here," Sneeds says, real puzzled like. He carries the broom to the back of the store and leans it up

246

against the other new brooms. "I'm awful sorry, Mrs. Johnson. I just saw it standing there and I thought it was yours. Let me give you your money back." He dings open the cash register. "There you go."

Mrs. Johnson got her purse out of her pocketbook, snapped it open, folded the bills and stuck them in and dropped the change in and clamped her purse shut and smiled at Sneeds. "I don't even need a broom," she says. "I got three."

Sneeds followed her to the door, saying he was sorry. But do you know what he did then? He walked to the back of the store, got that same broom and leaned it up against the cash register. *Again.*

"Sneeds Perry," I says, "you tried to cheat her."

"Oh, no. It was an honest mistake. I didn't mean to charge Mrs. Johnson for that broom."

"Well, Sneeds, you went and got it and set it right back up there! What for?"

"There's people, Raney, plenty of people—but not Mrs. Johnson—who come in here and charge stuff. Right?"

"Right."

"Well, some never pay it off. Paul Markham has a bill you wouldn't believe, and nobody knows about it but me and your daddy, and Paul'll pay *on* it, sure, but he won't pay it off. Well, it ain't right. It simply ain't right, and I tell your daddy and he won't do a thing about it. So,

I collect interest—I'll have a broom this week and a jar of pickles next week—one of them giant jars. Now that there with Mrs. Johnson was a accident. I didn't mean to ring up that broom. But Paul was in here yesterday and Fred Powers today and I'd just rung it up for both of them and so—"

"Sneeds, two wrongs don't make a right."

"I might as well get them both while they're here."

"No, no. I mean *your* wrong don't make *their* wrong right."

"Oh. Well, maybe not, but charging them extra ain't wrong because it cancels out their wrong. In other words, one wrong can cancel out another wrong."

"Sneeds. Sneeds, what if I tell Daddy? I mean I can't just ignore this."

"If you have to tell him, tell him. But I think you ought to remember that I agreed to you working in here in the first place, so if it hadn't been for me you wouldn't have known about this anyway, so it's my own doing, in a way. And what I'm doing is helping out your daddy, so you telling him would actually hurt him moneywise. But do what you have to do."

"Well, if it's something definitely wrong, like cheating, I'd have to tell him." I don't know what to do. I doubt Daddy would do anything. He's always making excuses for Sneeds.

4

WE HAVE TWO CARS. THE DODGE DART AND the Chevrolet Daddy gave me. The Chevrolet was in the shop yesterday and so Charles had to come get me at the store on his way home from the library. It's the only time he's picked me up in the three weeks I've been working there.

I'm in the back of the store when he walks in with Sneeds right behind him. He gets a Pepsi at about the same time I start up front. When he gets over to the cash register, where Sneeds is waiting, Sneeds reaches under the counter and pulls out this slick, shiny *Penthouse* magazine and slides it across to Charles at about the time Charles looks at me and I look down at the magazine and then right into Charles's eyes which are not looking back into mine but are instead staring at the cash register.

Sneeds rings up the magazine and the Pepsi and says, "Did you bring a bottle?"

"I don't want the magazine," Charles says, shaking his head.

"What's the problem?" says Sneeds, who, I all of a sudden realize, don't know that Charles is the Charles who is my Charles. Charles hardly ever goes in the store. *Or so I thought.* Live and learn.

Well, listen: I won't born yesterday. I just took

my pocketbook from underneath the counter, walked out front and got in the Dodge.

Charles comes out with*out* the magazine, drinking on that Pepsi. He comes up to the car window and do you know what he says? He says:

"Is there an empty bottle under your seat?"

"I don't know, Charles—there's no telling what might be under there. Where's your magazine? I came out so you could buy it."

"What magazine?"

Sneeds sticks his head out the store door. "I'm sorry, man, I swear. I am *sorr-y.*"

" '*What magazine?*' " I say to Charles. "That slick, shiny *Penthouse* magazine, full of filthy pictures of naked girls that Sneeds slid across the counter to you just as natural as . . . as . . . selling a . . . a . . . shiny red chicken to a black snake. *That's* what magazine."

"That's none of your business, Raney."

"Well, if it's none of my business, how come you clammed up like God was watching you?"

"I said it's none of your business. Don't change the subject."

"I swear, you must go in there as regular as meals to pick up a copy of that magazine. And Lord only knows where you hide them at home. Where *do* you hide them?"

"Raney, I said it's none of your business. It's absolutely none of your business. We happen to be living in a free country which tells me in its

250

own constitution that I am free to read what I want to, when I want to, without reporting in to you."

"If you're so free, Charles—where's the magazine?"

"I'll tell you one thing, Raney: it wouldn't hurt you to pick up a few pointers from *Penthouse*."

"Charles, you son of a . . . if you've got something to say to me then say it. Don't hide behind a stack of filthy magazines."

"Raney, they are not filthy magazines. Filth is in the mind of the beholder."

"You can say that again. And that's what I mean, Charles —you are filling your mind with filth."

"That's not what I'm talking about. I'm talking about how you define what you see. I do not define it as filth and you do define it as filth so what I'm saying is: speak for yourself."

See how he is. Here I am trying to say how I feel. That's what Dr. Bridges kept saying: "Get in touch with your feelings. Get in touch with your feelings and express them. You'll only be telling the truth." I know exactly how I feel about this magazine business but as soon as I express that to Charles, he gets off on some dictionary definitions. It's just like him. I'm concerned about this whole issue of sex in a consecrated marriage. How am I supposed to carry on a normal sex life with somebody who is reading these filthy magazines and coming up with no telling what in his mind. That was the whole problem on our honeymoon. I'll bet you five hundred dollars.

"Charles," I said, "the problem is this: I don't know what to do in a marriage that has this extra ingredient of filthy sex in it."

Charles didn't answer. He got in the car and we drove on home without saying one solitary word.

When we walked through the front door I said, "Charles, where do you keep all those filthy magazines?"

"Raney, it seems to me we could just leave this whole discussion off—cancel it, forget it."

"That would be fine with you, but what happens when you catch *me* doing something wrong?"

"Raney, you don't. . . ."

"What?"

"Don't you see that. . . . Listen, when I read one of those magazines, you tell me who is being hurt."

"First of all, Charles, you don't just read the magazine, you look at it."

"Okay, okay—whatever. What I want you to do is tell me who's getting hurt."

"Charles, the Bible warns against lusting in your heart. That's all I need to know about the subject. That's all I'm supposed to know about the subject. That's all I want to know about the subject. That's all there *is* to know about the subject."

"Raney, don't you see what that does to me? Don't you see how that leaves me without a chance to communicate anything about this to you? Don't you see there is no way I can talk to you now, and I have things inside me that I want to say—that I want to explain?"

I could tell he was serious. It seemed like he really did want to talk—like he needed to explain something, and Lord knows we're not all perfect, so:

"Okay, Charles," I said. "I'll listen. You go ahead and talk and I promise I'll listen." Dr. Bridges would have been proud.

"Raney, I can live a perfect sex life in my body, a faithful sex life. No problem. But not in my mind. Why did God give me this kind of mind if he—"

"Charles, you can't—"

"Raney, you *said* you would listen."

You know it's really hard to listen to somebody when they've got something completely wrong. It's almost like you want to mash them out, do away with them, clean them up.

"Okay," I said. "Go ahead."

"Well, for some reason—I guess because we reproduce biologically—I have an attraction for the opposite sex. I didn't put it there. It was there when I came along. Now what am I supposed to do with that?"

"Well. . . ."

"No, wait. That was a rhetorical question."

"I was just going to answer it."

"No, a rhetorical question doesn't need an answer."

"Then why do you call it a question? I never heard of a question that don't need a answer."

"It's a statement in question form."

"Well, why don't you just—"

"Wait a minute, Raney. Let me finish? Okay? Okay?"

"Okay."

"Now, I can't hide what flows around in my mind—and furthermore, I don't intend to. And I believe we should both be entitled to certain privileges of privacy. I believe that with all my heart, Raney. That does not mean anything about my soul going to hell. It does not mean anything about my having a filthy mind. It does not mean anything about my being unfaithful. It does not mean anything about committing adultery. It does not mean *anything* but that I am practicing my freedom, in a free country, with a God-given mind that has fantasies sometimes for God's sake."

"Charles, I don't think I can talk about this."

"Raney, please. I'm not asking you to talk about this. I'm asking you to listen. To try to understand my point of view. You don't have to agree. Listen, you don't have to agree with any of this. I'm asking you to try to understand something which you don't necessarily agree with. And that we can be different. We can be different about some things, Raney. It's okay. The world won't fall apart. If we could just agree to disagree and not get all bent out of shape. That was one of the main things we decided in therapy."

"I'm not all bent out of shape." I was thinking that if I could hold off, not get mad—go ahead and let Charles get all of this *out,* then maybe down the road somewhere we could solve the problem, and in the meantime, he'd have to listen to my views on all this. "I'm okay. I'm glad you're getting all this out, Charles. I think that's a good idea . . . and . . . Where do you keep all those filthy magazines?"

"Raney."

"Well?"

"Raney, I—"

"I just don't want to stumble over one of those filthy magazines some day when I'm looking for some reading material for our son or daughter."

"Raney, have you listened to—or heard— anything I've said?"

"I think so."

"I hope so."

I don't mind us disagreeing so much. It's just *what* we disagree over. And I do wish we could disagree over things it's *okay* to disagree over.

This sex business is one of the few areas in the universe, it seems to me, that we ought *not* to disagree over. What kind of car you want—okay. Whether to get the freezer on top or on the bottom of the refrigerator—okay. Whether or not to plant corn in the garden—okay. But there are some things. And sex is one of them. But I do think Charles and me have got to give each other a chance to talk about things. Next time he'll have to be quiet and listen to me. I did my part this time.

Some of what he said did make some sense somehow. I've just never thought about it along the lines of living in a free country.

5

THERE IS THIS HUSSY IN LISTRE—Thomasina Huggins. She lives five or six miles down Route 14 and she comes by the store about three times a week. Her husband left her and moved to Alaska. She's after Sneeds—anybody could tell—and I guess she's caught him.

Daddy gave me a key to the store in case I need to get in for any reason when it's closed. Last Saturday night, when I needed some eggs for Sunday morning, was just such an occasion. When I drove up I noticed Sneeds's pickup truck and Thomasina's black and orange Thunderbird parked around at the side of the store. The store closes at six on Saturdays, and it was about nine-fifteen when I pulled up.

Well, I'm not one to pry, but I absolutely had to have a dozen eggs. I unlocked the door and went in. I didn't try to be noisy and I didn't try to be quiet. The light from the street light was strong enough for me not to have to turn on the overhead light.

They were in the feed room. I heard them. And the light was on in there. The door was cracked. And the eggs happened to be by that door. So I *had* to see what they were doing. I couldn't help it.

They were sitting on three stacked bags of feed amongst all the other bags on the far side of the feed room with their feet on another bag and they had on *just their underpants* and were reading this magazine—just thumbing through it. It was one of those you-know-what magazines. And there was Thomasina's dinners just hanging there as big as day. I was absolutely shocked that something like this could be going on in my own daddy's store. I felt like I was in a trance. Her lipstick was as red as a candy apple and she had on dangly shiny ear rings. Tacky.

Sneeds poured her something out of a bottle into a *plastic cup* and she says, "Not too much, Sneeds," and giggles.

Well, what was I to do? I stepped—and the floor squeaked as loud as a creaking door. When

I lifted my foot it squeaked again. They looked in my direction and I started for the front door and said real loud and innocent, "Is anybody here?" There was nothing else to do. There was this scrambling and the feed room door slammed shut.

I hollered, "Sneeds, is that you?"

"Yes. It's me. Is that Raney?"

"Yes. I just had to come get a"—I looked to see what was close—"flashlight battery. See you later." And I got out of there. I had the eggs, too.

Well, I have never. Sneeds Perry, of all people. Who I work with. What could I do? Talk to Sneeds? Charles? Daddy? I didn't see how. Aunt Flossie? Dr. Bridges? I guessed not.

Well, Monday morning Sneeds acted nervous and jumpy. Who wouldn't? I didn't say one word. I didn't even look at him. I just went about my business, and at about ten A.M. when I'm back wiping off the drink box, he comes up behind me and says, "Did you know Thomasina Huggins and me are getting married?"

"Lord, no," I said, and kept polishing.

"Yep, we are. But we ain't told nobody."

I turned around and leaned up against the drink box.

"Yep," says Sneeds, "we were having a little engagement party when you came in Saturday night. But we don't want to tell anybody, so don't mention it yet."

258

Sneeds was lying bigger than a house. He wadn't a bit more engaged than me. He had had his fingers in the cookie jar that very weekend in the very feed room we were standing beside and was trying to mask it all over by lying to me about being engaged.

"Well, Sneeds, it's none of my business what you do in that feed room."

"What do you mean?" he says.

"Just that. It's okay whatever you do."

"Did you look in there Saturday night?"

"In where?"

"In the *feed* room."

"I certainly didn't." I felt my cheeks and neck getting hot. "Sneeds, I'm real happy you're getting married and I just suppose I think a feed room is an unusual place to have an engagement party." I started wiping the drink box again—with my back to it.

"Well, the truth is, Raney—we keep a little bottle back there and we just stopped by for a little harmless nip. And I'll tell you something else: you only live once."

All this was too much. I got the conversation stopped, went back to polishing the drink box, and Sneeds went back up front.

Engagement party my foot. It was a party all right, but not an engagement party. They were having a mighty good time and it came back to me about what Charles had said about nobody getting hurt making something all right. Just because nobody is getting hurt does not make something right. Nobody was getting hurt when Hitler *started* making speeches before World War II or when the Japanese were *on their way* to Pearl Harbor.

If Sneeds and Thomasina had been married, maybe it would have been different.

Monday night I'd decided to talk to Charles about the whole incident when Sandra and Bobby Ferrell (who've been saying they were coming to see us) knocked on the door.

Charles gets furious when somebody decides to just drop by and he refuses to go see anybody unless they know for sure he's coming. I say that takes all the surprise out of it, which is one of the best parts of a visit anyway. Charles thinks it has to do with manners and he can't understand that since Sandra and Bobby were raised around here they don't have all these insights into Emily Post that he has. And never will, or want to, or should have.

Anyway, they came on in and sat down and asked us to sing a song. We sang a bluegrass arrangement of "Bless Be the Tie that Binds" which I worked up last week. We both like it and plan to start finishing all our gigs with it.

When we finished, Bobby and Sandra clapped. Then Bobby started asking Charles questions

like he was getting to know him. He asked
Charles if he ever did any hunting. I've heard
Charles talk about hunting just enough to know
he don't like it.

"No, I can't say as I have," said Charles.
"Never had the heart to."

"Never had the heart to?" says Bobby.

"That's right. Never had the heart to."

"Well, the way I always look at it," says
Bobby—"Do you eat chicken?"

"Yeah, I eat chicken," says Charles.

"Well, the way I always look at it is this:
somebody has to kill the chicken, and the
chicken is meat and the way I look at it is—I
might as well kill my own meat. I mean what's
the difference?"

"Well, the difference is—"

"I mean it all comes out the same."

"Well, I'd never thought about it exactly that
way. I think—"

"Most people don't. I mean if a person
absolutely refuses to eat meat for some reason
then I don't have no argument, because it's a fact
that I do eat meat and if they don't, I can
understand them being against killing it. It's just
that if *I* eat it, then I don't see that it makes no
difference who kills it—me or the butcher."

"I don't have any problem with eating it," says
Charles, "but I think I would have some problem
shooting it—whatever it is: a squirrel or

something. The idea of my taking away life just happens to bother me."

"Charles," I said, "you don't seem to mind catching fish. That's not exactly logical is it? You're taking away a fish's life as much as a squirrel's."

"It bothers me more with animals because—"

"Wait a minute," says Bobby, and laughs. "Animals kill each other, you know."

"People kill each other!" says Charles. "That doesn't mean I'm supposed to kill people!"

I was getting embarrassed. Here was Charles already raising his voice, but on the other hand I could see why. I realized I hadn't ever talked to Bobby very much—or he hadn't ever talked to me very much. He was insisting too hard on this subject of hunting all of a sudden; and in a way I didn't blame Charles for raising his voice. I couldn't figure out exactly what Bobby was getting at.

Daddy asked Charles to go hunting once and Charles said no and that's all that was ever said about it. I figured I ought to say something on Charles's behalf:

"But, Bobby, what if you don't like to shoot things that are alive?"

"Well, not only do these animals, and fish, kill each other for a purpose, unlike people—I mean hawks killing quail and rabbits and stuff—but you've got the natural environment doing the same thing. I mean flash floods and so forth wipe out millions of animals a year. And another thing: money from hunting licenses helps preserve wildlife, which is one of the reasons it's good to hunt."

Charles was getting fidgety, so I tried to remind Bobby what I was talking about. "But what if you don't like to shoot things that are alive? Charles don't like to shoot things that are alive and I don't think I would either, even though my daddy does it."

"Well, have you ever shot a quail on the wing?" Bobby says to me.

"I never shot one anywhere."

"No, I mean flying."

"No, I never even shot a rifle."

"You don't shoot a quail with a rifle. You use a shotgun."

"Oh, no, I never have and I don't think I'd want to. I feel like Charles in that respect. We've talked about it before."

"Well. Whatever. But there's a great deal of sportsmanship and marksmanship involved. I mean you have to have very good reflexes, and good eyesight, and be very quick."

"You're probably in the NRA," says Charles.

"That's right," says Bobby.

"What's the difference between having good reflexes and being quick?" I said. I didn't know what the "NRA" had to do with it.

"Well, with reflexes you're speaking about accuracy, and with quickness you're talking about speed. But I mean, really, each to his own. I guess I just see it as a sport and darn exciting at times and a way to put meat on the table, unless of course you're some weirdo vegetarian or something."

I looked at Charles, wondering if he'd say it. Charles looked at me. "Charles's mother is a vegetarian," I said. "But she ain't weirdo."

I must say I felt right good about that. Bobby shrugged his shoulders and looked like he was looking with his eyes for something to say. I just hadn't ever talked to Bobby and I hadn't realized he'd be so insistent. Sandra came in on our side—at least more on our side than on Bobby's:

"What I can't stand," she said, "is *cleaning* quail. Bobby expects me to clean them. He'll come in and—"

"You don't clean your own game?" says Charles.

"Well, I clean them sometimes."

"When did you ever clean the first bird?" says Sandra. She was looking at Bobby like she didn't like him.

Bobby was getting a little fidgety now. "I've cleaned them before." He looked at Sandra like he could shoot *her.* I noticed that that was the first time he'd looked at her at *all.*

"Well, I can't remember when," says Sandra.

"Your daddy is a big hunter," I said to Sandra. She certainly deserved a right to be included.

"Oh, yes. He's been hunting with your daddy before, and he goes with Sneeds Perry right much—the one who works out at your daddy's store."

"Do you know if Sneeds is engaged?" I said.

"No. I hadn't heard. Why?"

"I just wondered. I guess I ought to ask him. I'm working part time out at the store now and I was just wondering. Somebody said something about it."

"How do you like working out there?"

I went on to talk about the store for a while. They didn't stay a whole lot longer and I must admit I understood a little more about how Charles could feel about Bobby.

When they left me and Charles laughed about how Bobby's face looked when I said Charles's mother was a vegetarian. And I felt a little bit sorry for Sandra—for how she's bound to feel left out sometimes. I asked Charles if he noticed and he said he did.

I forgot to bring up about the feed room until we were going to bed, but then I decided not to—in case it developed into a long conversation with Charles going on and on about his views on all this sex and so forth.

265

6

WELL, HERE'S HOW THIS FEED ROOM business turned out. My soul is still reeling about the whole thing. I've prayed about it, with some success, I suppose.

Two nights ago, Thursday, me and Charles were driving back from supper at the Ramada Inn and I had to get a half gallon of milk. It was about eight and the store was closed.

Something I must explain first is this: Charles has got me to sip his white wine at the Ramada a few times—to show me how much better it makes the food taste. One night I tried a whole glass. Just to make the food taste better because it can make the food taste some better, depending on what you're eating. Thursday night when we stopped by the store I'd had *two* glasses. For the first time. I don't think I'll ever do it again, and I shouldn't have then. I can't decide what I think about it exactly. It does make the food taste some better.

Charles followed me into the store and I got the milk and while I was leaving a IOU note by the cash register I told Charles about seeing Sneeds and Thomasina in the feed room. Being there in the store helped me tell about it.

Charles walks on back to the feed room and turns on the light and starts looking around. I followed him.

Well, I don't know how to explain what happened. What happened to me inside. It was like something was melting to a gold-yellow color—and I just don't know how to explain this, but I wanted to sit on a feed bag in my underwear. I don't know where it all came from, unless from the very Devil himself, but I thought to myself: Charles and me are married. There's nothing in the Bible about what married people can't do together. It's a free country.

But I don't know how to explain this feeling inside me. It seemed like such a cozy room. It was warm and those feed bags had this smell which was kind of musky, and they had this rough texture, and Charles found the magazine and I felt as awful as I've ever felt in my life but at the same time just as good. Honest. Both together.

I decided to go with the good. I didn't say a word.

"Here's the magazine," Charles said, "and the booze—Southern Comfort."

I didn't say a word. I walked over to Charles and he looked at me and he must have seen what was happening inside me because he just simply gave me this little kiss on the lips and let it linger for a while longer than it should have and I wasn't thinking about what was going on in his head, but what was happening inside me and it was like I had to give over my insides to the

Devil but I couldn't fight it and for heaven's sake we are married I said to myself.

"Charles, let's sit down. My knees are a little weak."

Charles's cheeks were flushed. I can always tell.

So we sat on that tight bag of feed and Lord have mercy I did want my *bare* fanny on it and Charles says:

"Now Raney, you just relax. I want you to see that . . . look, there are stories in here, and advertisements and—"

And I'm sitting there wanting to take my skirt *and panties* off for heaven's sake, and I don't care what's in the magazine. Charles and me are married. So:

I stood up and Charles stopped thumbing through the magazine and everything was melting inside and jumping around getting excited and I said to myself "Lord, please excuse me for a minute." And that almost broke what was happening inside but it came right back so I figured the Lord had done so: excused me—and Charles was looking up at me like he didn't know *what* to expect. So I just—very slowly, to get it right, to give it the best effect which would fit what was going on inside me—I just unbuttoned the three buttons down the side of my skirt, slowly, and let my eyes droop to about half mast, and let the skirt drop, and then popped the elastic on my panties and pulled them right off over my ankles and put my warm fanny down beside Charles on that tight, rough feed bag and said:

"Hand me a warm-up of Southern Comfort, Charles—my fanny's getting cold."

And after that it was me, Charles, and the feedbags. And I'd just had my hair done that afternoon. But I didn't pay a bit of mind to that. I was happy and it was wonderful.

I've reconciled myself to it.

7

I'M PREGNANT. DR. LEWIS TOLD ME LAST Wednesday. One year after we got married. I can't believe it. I'm going to have a little baby. My prayers have been answered. I thought I might be, so Charles got a home pregnancy test from the drug store and it came out positive. Dr. Lewis confirmed it.

We decided two or three months ago for Charles to stop using preventatives and I just had no idea from what all Madora and me talked about that it would happen so soon.

Lord have mercy, it might have happened in the *feed room.*

I think I want a little girl. I helped with Mary Faye and Norris, and Mary Faye was the easiest. And my cousins who have babies—Betty, Jake, the other Betty, Mary Beth, and Julia—have little girls who are so much cuter, and behave so much better than the little boys. The little boys seem to have something sour and hard under their skins. The little girls are so different, sweet and soft somehow, except for Mary Beth's little girl, Bonnie. She's been spoiled to death. To death. If she don't get something she wants she simply starts crying and then waits for her mother to tell her three times to be quiet. Then on the fourth time, whatever it is she wants, she gets. I declare if that child wanted to ride on top of the car in the rain, you could look out your window and there she'd come—riding on top of the car in the rain.

The thing is—it's not her fault. It's her mama's and daddy's fault. They follow her around and tell her it's okay to go ahead and do whatever it is she wants to do. Oh, they might put up a little fuss, but by and large she gets exactly what she wants with only very slight delays once in a while. She knows the exact little pout or cry that will get her what she wants. They let her make her own *decisions*. I say a very small child don't have enough brain material to make decisions, most decisions. Plus, children have to learn that *they* have to adjust to the world and not the world to them. And I want you to know that when that child knocked over and broke a flower vase in my living room, that child's mother,

Mary Beth, did not get up from where she was sitting, did not say she was sorry, did not say one word. Sat there munching on a chocolate chip cookie, talking about politics. But: *that* little girl is an exception.

I'm just thankful I had all that experience helping out with Mary Faye and Norris.

Charles is excited too. He's been as sweet as can be since we found out. He's started to cook lots more. Bless his heart. To help me out, plus I think he enjoys it. His fried okra is as good as Mama's.

We had some French onion soup at the mall and Charles said he knew he could do better so he bought some onions and cheese and a can of onion soup and a can of cream of onion soup and drained off the water from the straight onion soup and mixed it with the cream of onion and added chopped onions and cheese and cold toast and it was pretty good. I told him to send the idea to Campbell Soup. They have little recipes on the soup cans all the time.

His main problem with cooking is that he leaves the stove eyes on after he's finished, and like I said: the drain strainer out of the sink so that gobs of raw cabbage and such can get down in there and stop it up, and the faucet turned on, wasting water.

Last Saturday, our commode got stopped up and the plumber's friend wouldn't do no good so we called Mr. Nelson and he came and worked and worked and finally had to take the whole commode up out of the floor. He said he wanted to get home to watch the Braves on TV (he knows Daddy—that's why he came on Saturday) and I know the game had already started when he pulled out—from below floor level—this cabbage core. About the size of your fist.

Now I knew *I* hadn't dropped a cabbage core down the commode.

My mama told me never to drop anything down the commode that did not come from your own body. Nothing, absolutely nothing—except toilet paper, of course.

This is one of the rules she lives by.

Why in the world Charles walked all the way into the bathroom with that cabbage core and dropped it into the commode is something I'll never understand.

So I said, "Charles, why in the world you walked all the way into the bathroom with that cabbage core and dropped it into the commode is something I'll never understand."

He said he did it, and that he was sorry and wouldn't do it again. I should hope not. There's no telling what all he's thrown down that commode, maybe other cabbage cores. I think he's learned his lesson now though. Mr. Nelson was mighty perturbed and told Charles straight out that dropping a cabbage core down a commode is a dumb thing to do and that he'd probably already missed a good portion of the ball game.

The cooking Charles does will certainly help out after we have the baby. One thing about it is: he won't take no advice on cooking at all—none at all. Sometimes he thinks he's Julia Child.

Like he asked this guy, Tom Rubin, from the library, and his girlfriend, Marilyn, to eat supper with us last Friday night. Charles told me he was going to cook a good Southern meal because Tom is from New York.

So I asked what I could do to help and he says, "Nothing, Raney, absolutely nothing. I want to do it all myself."

Friday afternoon he gets home with squash, fresh corn, snap beans, and okra from Daddy's garden and chicken from the Piggly Wiggly. Well, I figured I'd help out just a little bit. Not enough to count. So I put a little water in the pot for the vegetables. You need very little water in the pot for vegetables—vegetables of any kind. Unless you want them soggy. You don't want them raw, like at restaurants, but you don't want them absolutely soggy either.

So, I put a little water in a pot for the corn, a little water in a pot for the snap beans, and a little water in the frying pan to start up some squash and onions.

Charles comes in the kitchen and practically shouts, "Raney, what are you doing?"

"I'm just helping with a couple of little things for supper."

"Number one," he says, "I'm fixing *dinner*. *You* fix *supper*. *I* fix *dinner*. And a number two: I'm doing this alone if you don't mind."

"Well, of course I don't mind," I says. "I just know how nice it is to have a little help in the kitchen once in a while."

I was shaving the corn kernels off the cob because Charles said he was having stewed corn.

"What in the world are you doing that for?" he asks.

"You said you wanted stewed corn, didn't you?"

"Why are you cutting it off the ear?"

"Because that's the way you fix stewed corn."

"No, it's not."

This really took the cake. I'd been watching my mother fix stewed corn for over twenty years and suddenly here's Charles—a librarian, and a man—telling me how to fix stewed corn. "Well, how do *you* fix stewed corn, Mr. Chef Boy Are Dee?"

"You boil it on the cob and then you cut it off."

That was like somebody telling me you cook string beans in a peach pie. Charles was getting too big for his pants.

"No, you don't, Charles. You cut it off first.

Call Mama if you don't believe me. Then you put it in a pot with a little water, salt, a pinch of sugar—"

"Raney. Just let me do this."

Here's Charles with a chance to learn something from me about cooking. And what does he do? He tries to do it all. Won't listen to a word I say. I told him he had too much water for the snap beans. You don't need more than a half cup. Then if you need more later, you add it. Charles uses water like a sieve. He runs enough water in the tub to float. I try to save water.

Finally he really did get mad. He was going to brown these brown and serve rolls in the toaster oven. I know for a fact that they're better if they're browned in the stove oven. He had them sitting over by the toaster, so I said, "Are you going to brown those in there?"

He got real mad. "Raney, somehow your brain doesn't program the fact that I want to fix this meal by myself. If it turns out awful and I do it myself, I'll be overjoyed. If it turns out perfect and you helped, I'll go crazy. I *am* going crazy. Please don't tell me where to brown the rolls, how much water to use, what temperature to cook the chicken with. Please."

I had not said one thing about what temperature to cook the chicken with.

"Charles, I don't think I should be shouted at while I'm pregnant."

I came on back to the living room and read the Want Ads. Maybe I overdid it. But I was only trying to help.

This Tom Rubin who came over for supper was a Jew. I wouldn't have known if they hadn't started talking about it at the supper table. (The supper was pretty good. Too much water in the snap beans and the chicken was dry. But I didn't say anything. I take credit for not saying anything. Aunt Flossie has told me several times about how she finally learned not to say anything about Uncle Frank's bird dogs.)

Tom's girlfriend, Marilyn, is not a Jew and we got to talking about babies and marriage. Tom mentioned how his mother and daddy felt about Marilyn. I couldn't believe they didn't like her simply because she was a regular American, and that they didn't want them to get married on account of it. I can't imagine that.

They were both real nice—he didn't seem like a Jew at all. I guess I haven't really met that many. They raved about the meal. Charles had insisted we serve wine so I got a big bottle at the Winn Dixie. I bought a loaf of bread to cover it up in case I saw somebody I knew. We had some left over and I'm saving it for cooking. It's good on fish.

After they left, while Charles was cleaning up, he turned on the faucet and left it on, with the strainer out of the sink. I put it back in and said,

"Charles, I think we ought to save as much water as we can now that the baby's coming."

"I don't want that strainer in there," says Charles. He took the strainer back out.

"Why?"

"I don't wash dishes that way."

"I don't see why you don't put water in the sink and then put soap in the water and then put the dishes in."

"I do it differently, Raney."

"Why?"

"I just do it differently, that's all. I don't like to wash dishes in dirty water."

"Dirty water?"

"I don't like to get gunk in the dishwater and then keep washing dishes as if nothing happened."

"Charles, it does not work that way, and you know it."

"Yes, it does."

"You rinse them off with hot water first. Besides, dishwater don't get that dirty, and besides that, Charles, food's not dirty. What makes you think food is dirty?"

"Raney, if you want to wash your dishes with tomato sauce and little bits of meat and grease floating all around in the water, then go ahead, but I'm not about to."

"Think about how much water you're wasting. You run enough water in there to take a shower in."

"I just won't take a shower on the days I wash dishes."

"Well, I can't make you wash dishes the way I do, but—"

"No, you can't."

"I think it's a waste of water."

"Do you think America is going to fall to the communists, Raney? Over this? Are we going to dry up and blow away? Will there be no tomorrow?"

"Well, I—"

"No, don't answer."

What I want to know is how can you take a hardheaded man and teach him the right way to do something in the kitchen?

And it's not much different out in the yard. Take Mr. Edmonds next door. He has this tool shed with all these yard tools and things and he has a garden every year. Not Charles.

But on the other hand, I don't suppose Mr. Edmonds cooks, and then too, there is Charles's mental ability and his potential and all.

I went to bed while Charles was still cleaning up in the kitchen and about time I got settled in good, I heard Charles talking on the phone to Johnny Dobbs and of all the things in the world: Charles was asking him did he want to be our baby's *godfather!* I don't know what a godfather is supposed to do, but if a black gets legally kin to my family, we'll have to move to Hawaii.

Charles and me will just have to have a heart to heart talk about it. I'll have to explain about how it is. And I'll have to tell him about the vent so he'll understand that I was not intentionally listening in.

8

THIS PREGNANCY HAS BEEN THE MOST amazing thing—five months now, and I've been through different stages of feelings about it all. I had a nightmare right away during the first month. There was this tiny mean thing in a black hood and it came in the night to the foot of the bed and rose up and said in a raspy voice, "I'm going to kill you, Randy." It called me Randy. And it started for my stomach and I grabbed to push it away and got my hands tangled in the covers and the covers were the monster so even after I was awake I was still screaming and pushing at it. Charles was holding me, telling me everything was okay and for a minute I thought *he* was after me too.

It was the worst thing in the world. When I got straightened out I was all weak and shaky and out of breath. Charles turned on the light and we sat in bed and talked. He hadn't figured out that I was nervous to death about this baby, this live thing, in my stomach—that it had given me a secret tremors that I hadn't been able to talk about. We sat there in the bed and talked about it and I felt so much better. Charles said any kind of feelings were normal and that if I was scared it was for one of the best reasons in the world. I'd been trying to push back the thought of maybe I don't want this baby, especially when on the day I found out I was happier than any day of my life. It didn't fit together.

What it all came down to is I was trying so hard to feel what I was supposed to feel I mashed down all the real feelings and then they sprung up in that nightmare. I suppose that's what happened. That's what me and Charles finally figured out sitting up in bed. But Lord knows what Mother and Aunt Naomi would think if they found out I had thought about not wanting a baby.

Other than that, my body has been going through changes which Charles and me have read are normal. He's found some real good books about all this. I'm gaining weight; I *love* to smell leather all of a sudden; I'm getting these little urges—I took the doors off the kitchen cabinets and it makes things so much nicer in there. If you live in a house where the cabinet doors come open and pop you in the head, then you should just take them all off. Spice cans and vegetable cans are right colorful—especially if you get canned tomatoes. We've got curtains on the kitchen windows that match tomato cans and Campbell soup cans.

The other thing is I get constipated all the time and feel like I have the flu in the afternoons. But the nice thing is I'm not sick in the mornings.

Saturday night I came into the kitchen for a drink of water and Charles says, "When the baby's born don't you think we ought to have it baptized?" Well, that surprised me to death. It's common sense that a baby don't need baptizing. A baby can't think, so how in the world could a baby make a decision about Jesus? But the main reason not to have our baby baptized is that Free Will Baptists do not have babies baptized.

"Charles," I says, "that's something Catholics and Methodists and Episcopalians do. Free Will Baptists don't baptize babies. Besides, what the others do is sprinkle, even though it says in the Bible as plain as your face, 'when Jesus came up out of the water.'"

"Raney, Free Will Baptists are not the only denomination recognized in America."

"I certainly don't want to get anything done to our baby that's not done at Bethel Free Will Baptist. Where would you have her baptized?"

"Her?"

"Well, whatever."

"At the Episcopal church in White Level."

"Charles, did your mother get you started on this?"

"No, my mother did not get me started on this."

281

"Well, that's not my church so I can't see getting my own flesh and blood baptized over there."

"I'm thinking about joining," Charles says. "And I'd like for you to think about it too. Wait a minute. Just think about it."

I was flabbergasted. I never dreamed of such a thing. I didn't see how I could consider such a thing; and the prospects of him going to that rich Episcopal church and me going to Bethel Free Will Baptist and a dear child growing up in the middle of that split was almost too much for me to bear.

"Charles, you can't go to a Episcopal church. They're against some of the very things we believe in most."

"What do you mean by that, Raney?"

"We talked about this with your mother."

"Oh."

"Sometime before the baby's born we need to sit down and have a long talk about this whole thing."

"Okay. I'll listen if you will."

We're having a good time at Sunday dinners over at Mama's. We take our instruments and play music. Norris is learning some banjo from Charles and I'm teaching Mary Faye a few guitar chords. Charles just learned "Soldier's Joy" on the banjo. I don't know why he hadn't learned it before. I play it on the record player all the time—it's on the Circle Album. It's the best instrumental recording I've ever heard. Frailing and three-finger picking together. It works on your insides. I listen to it five times straight sometimes.

Mama and Aunt Naomi have been coming up with names for the baby. Mama bought a book with two hundred real cute names and every Sunday she comes up with three or four. Aunt Naomi dug up all the family names reaching back into the 1800's. She wrote them all down and circled the ones she likes best. I've been waiting for Charles to complain.

When I go to bed at night, the baby wakes up and kicks; it feels like a rabbit trying to kick out of your hand.

Yesterday I worked my last day at the store, until well after the baby's born, anyway. Charles likes Johnny Carson and he sat up to watch some of that. The baby was still kicking when he finally came to bed.

"Charles, put your hand on there."

"I'll be damned," he says. He says that every time he feels the baby kick.

"I'll bet its little footsies are about a inch long," I said.

"Footsies?"

"Yes, footsies."

"Raney, they are feet. *Feet,* not footsies. What are you going to call its breasts?"

"Well, I'm certainly not going to call them 'breasts.' That's for a grown woman."

"What *are* you going to call them?"

"I'm going to call them the same thing my mother called them: ninny-pies."

"*Ninny-pies.* Raney, what in the world?"

"What's wrong with 'ninny-pies,' for heaven's sake?"

"Raney, that's the dumbest thing I've ever heard."

"Well, it won't too dumb for my mother and her mother and on back down the line to England."

"Raney, I don't want my little girl growing up telling her best friend that she just bought her first brassiere for her 'ninny-pies.'"

"By then maybe she'll be calling them 'dinners.'"

"Oh, no. Raney, please."

Charles has no imagination, sometimes. He'd rather call things by their book names. "Charles," I said, "there's nothing wrong with that. It's what I grew up with."

"Raney, if what you grew up with was all right for everyone, the world would be quite different."

"I'll say. And for the better."

"What are you going to call the baby's natural functions?"

"'Natural functions?'"

"Going to the bathroom: urinating and defecating."

"'Defecating?'"

"Taking a crap, Raney."

"Well, I'm certainly not going to ask a two-year-old girl with pigtails if she has to go 'take a crap.'"

"What will you ask her?"

"I'll ask her if she wants to go grunt."

"Go *grunt?* Go *grunt?* Raney that's ridiculous."

"Ridiculous? It certainly is not. What would you say?"

"Well, I don't know; this is not one of the things I've planned out. Maybe I should have. What have you got for urinate?"

"Wee-wee. What else is there?"

"That's what I figured. How about if we compromise and come up with 'pee?'"

"I think we ought to start out with 'wee-wee' and when she gets a little older, 'pee-pee,' and then finally 'pee.'"

"Are you going to start out with 'gruntie-gruntie' and work up to 'grunt?'"

"Well . . . that doesn't sound like such a bad—"

"*Raney,* I wasn't serious."

"Well, I think you should be serious. This is serious business. We have to call all those things something. And my family must have put a lot of thought into this sort of thing."

"I'll say."

"Well, I haven't heard you come up with a single thing yet but 'breast.' Why can't we use our God-given imaginations and come up with something that's not so shocking when we talk about it. When I was growing up I could talk about going to the bathroom in front of whoever I wanted to and nobody batted a eyelash."

"You know why nobody batted an eyelash, Raney?"

"Why?"

"Because they didn't know what the hell you were talking about."

Then Charles got into something about euphoniums or something and finally drifts off to sleep. But he had this little whistle going in his nose which got louder and louder until I finally woke him up and told him to turn over. He turned over but the whistle kept going. I don't know what time I finally did get to sleep. But I slept late the next morning. Charles was real quiet when he got up.

JUNE 20, 1977

FROM THE *Hansen County Pilot*:

BETHEL—Thurman "Ted" William Shepherd, born February 24 in Oakview Hospital and baptized yesterday at St. John's Episcopal Church in White Level, is the son of Mr. and Mrs. Charles Shepherd of 209 Catawba Drive in Listre. Charles is the head librarian at Listre Community College, while Mrs. Shepherd is a housewife.

Mr. and Mrs. Thurman Bell, of Bethel, the maternal grandparents, were in attendance. Mrs. Bell gave a reception in the Bethel Free Will Baptist Church education building following the baptism.

The paternal grandparents, Dr. and Mrs. William Shepherd from Atlanta, Georgia, were also in attendance and are spending the week with Charles, Raney, and Ted in their home in Listre.

Mrs. Madora Bryant, of Bethel, was named godmother. Mr. Johnny Dobbs, from New Orleans, was named godfather and is visiting for a few days. He is staying at the Ramada Inn.